ANIMAL PHANTOMS
TRUE GHOST STORIES

BARBARA SMITH

GHOST
HOUSE

Ghost House Books

© 2004 by Ghost House Books
First printed in 2004   10 9 8 7 6 5 4 3 2 1
Printed in Canada

The Publisher: Ghost House Books
Distributed by Lone Pine Publishing
10145 – 81 Avenue   1808 – B Street NW, Suite 140
Edmonton, AB T6E 1W9   Auburn, WA 98001
Canada   USA

Website: http://www.ghostbooks.net

Library and Archives Canada Cataloguing in Publication

Smith, Barbara, 1947–
    Animal phantoms : true ghost stories / Barbara Smith.

    Includes bibliographical references.
    ISBN 1-894877-52-7

    1. Animal ghosts—Juvenile literature.   I. Title.

BF1484.S54 2004   j398.25   C2004-903436-7

Editorial Director: Nancy Foulds
Project Editors: Shelagh Kubish, Chris Wangler
Illustrations and Cover Image: Aaron Norell
Production Manager: Gene Longson
Book Design, Layout and Production: Curtis Pillipow
Cover Design: Gerry Dotto, Curtis Pillipow

We acknowledge the financial support of the Government of Canada through the Book Publishing Industry Development Program (BPIDP) for our publishing activities.

PC: P6

For Nicholas, Danny and Emily
Here's to "spirited" lives

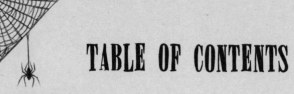

TABLE OF CONTENTS

NOTE FROM THE AUTHOR

What exactly is a ghost? Does anyone really know? Believe it or not, it's actually much easier to say what a ghost isn't than to say what it is.

For instance, we know for certain that a real ghost is not a smiling little white cartoon figure. Nor is a ghost necessarily something you can see. You can't always tell just by looking around whether a place is haunted or not. Even if you can't see anything unusual at all, a ghost might still be present.

A ghost is not always a scary thing. Judging from true ghost stories, most phantoms do not walk about moaning and dragging chains around with them. That's just what made-up stories try to have us believe, like the white cartoon figure.

If these are some of the things that ghosts are not, then is there also a list of what they really are? A quick look through any of the books in the Ghost House Books series will tell you that these mysterious creatures come in all shapes, sizes and personalities.

Some ghosts are apparitions—ghosts that you can see. Others will make their presence known as odors or as sounds. And then there are noisy poltergeists— that like to move things around.

Some ghosts only appear at predictable times. The ghost of Canadian artist Tom Thomson, who died in July 1917, is only seen on the anniversary of his death.

A few well-documented ghosts haunt only one specific place during the afterlife. Anne Boleyn's phantom has haunted the Tower of London, and nowhere else, ever since she was executed there on the orders of her husband, King Henry VIII, way back in 1536!

Another kind of ghost haunts the living on a less "permanent" basis. Some spirits return for a particular reason. These souls are called "crisis apparitions" or "forerunners." Their appearance, as we shall see, seems to predict something—and usually not something good—about the future.

But the big question is whether ghosts have to be the spirits of once-living people. Can there also be ghosts of animals? Although I've collected thousands of true ghost stories over the years, I never would have thought that the spirit of an animal could stay behind on earth—until my own cat, P.J., died.

Every night after dinner my family used to go downstairs and relax. Every night P.J. would join us, always choosing someone's lap to sit on. For three nights after our dependable little pet died, I could hear her ghostly paws on the stairs as she began to make her way down to join us. In death, her phantom paws never made it to the bottom step. The ghostly sounds faded away after the first six steps. After four nights we never heard the patter of her spectral little paws again.

I've always hoped that P.J. had found her way to her next happy life, because that little cat's ghost first alerted me to the possibility that the spirits of animals might occasionally return to roam the earth. After researching and writing the stories for this book, I don't wonder about that possibility quite as much.

Instead I wonder what you might think as you curl up to read the animal ghost stories I've chosen to re-tell here. There's no need to be scared—well not too much anyway. Most of the ghosts in this book didn't hurt the people they encountered, except to frighten them half to death of course. So keep your spirits up and enjoy your adventure into the animal beyond!

Hauntingly yours,
Barbara Smith

TANK TERROR

When 11-year-old Michael Tandy heard that his entire family was moving to England from Ireland, he was not impressed. His father had taken a teaching job at a private school near London and Mike was going to have to leave the town where he had lived all his life. When he heard what his father had to say, he was even less impressed.

"It'll be great, Mike," his father said. "I'll be home every day for lunch because we'll be living in a big old house right on the school grounds."

Yeah, right, Michael thought with a heavy heart. *If anything could possibly be lamer than being a teacher's son, it had to be living in a schoolyard.* Even though he didn't say anything, at that very moment Mike had a sudden sinking feeling. Little did he know how deadly accurate that sensation would turn out to be.

On the day the moving truck arrived, it was pouring rain. *It figures*, Michael grumbled to himself. But by the end of the day, even Mike had to admit that everything had gone quite well. The worst part had definitely been getting his tiny tropical fish ready for the trip. He had dozens and dozens of them and their water-filled home was a huge, rectangular aquarium. When the tank was filled with water and fish, it weighed twice as much as Mr. Tandy!

Michael learned what he had to do to get the fish and their home from the family's house in Ireland to their new one in England. Shipping tropical fish is complicated because they are very delicate creatures and any sudden change in their water could kill them all.

It was a lot of work and there was not much time to do it, so Michael's mother helped get the fish ready for their journey. They filled a smaller container full of water from the large aquarium. Then, one at a time, Mike caught the fish in a special net and carefully transferred them into the container. Once all the fish had been moved, the boy and his mother drained the rest of the water and cleaned the tank thoroughly.

The movers could now easily handle the empty glass tank, and the fish, in their smaller, temporary home, could make the trip to England with Mike and his family.

Needless to say, Mike was very relieved when his delicate fish arrived safely at his new home. As soon as the movers had gone, he wanted to get his fish back into their regular tank right away.

"Whoa," his mother replied. "You of all people should know that it'll take a few days to get the aquarium ready for them. We have to fill it and then let the water settle for a couple of days."

By lunchtime the next day, Michael had unpacked for himself and had helped his parents unpack. He could then fill the fish tank and set up the special air pump and water heater that prepared the water for his varieties of fish.

The following weekend, when he was sure that everything worked properly, Michael placed the smaller, temporary fish tank into the larger one. Then he stood back and watched as the colorful little fish swam back into their original "home sweet home," which rested on a specially built table in the living room near the fireplace. As soon as he saw that they were settled in all right, Michael felt a lot better.

Perhaps he too would settle in equally well and maybe he'd lose his crazy thought that something bad was going to happen.

One evening a few weeks later, Michael was babysitting his four-year-old sister Mary Beth when his parents were both out. Mary Beth was already in bed and he was sitting in the big easy chair reading by the fireplace. All was quiet. For the time being, the book had his attention.

Slowly, Mike began to feel just a little bit uncomfortable—like he was no longer alone in the room. Goose bumps traveled up and down his spine. The hairs on his arms were standing straight up. Tiny feathers of air tickled the back of his neck and his stomach felt cold and hard inside. Michael was terrified.

Something, or someone, was close to him. He couldn't see or hear anything but he was certain, absolutely certain, that something bad was some-where in the room with him. A moment later, he realized that the invisible presence was near the fish tank. He also sensed that the presence was evil.

Summoning up all his courage, Michael Tandy stood up. He heard a strange noise and looked toward the door to the living room. He watched in horror as, ever so slowly, the door opened just a bit wider than it had been. Then he could hear someone climbing the stairs to the second story of the house. Into his terrified mind jumped the thought, *Mary Beth is alone up there in her bedroom!*

Mike knew he had to do something, but what? It took a moment, but he finally rallied some self-control and ran to the bottom of the staircase. He could hear the thud of a footfall on each step as the invisible intruder made its way up the stairs. Mike could still see absolutely nothing on the stairs, despite the sound of footsteps.

Soaked with perspiration, Mike ran up the stairs two at a time. Even if he couldn't see what the danger was, he had to protect his sister. As he got to the sixth step on the staircase, he stumbled and nearly fell. It felt as though he'd brushed against someone. The boy stifled a scream and dashed the rest of the way into Mary Beth's bedroom.

To his relief, everything was all right. Mary Beth was fast asleep.

Whatever it is, it must be hiding somewhere, Michael thought. He took a big breath and began to search every nook and cranny of the second floor of the house.

He found nothing.

No one.

The place was completely empty—except for Mike, Mary Beth and whatever he had brushed past on the stairs. Still terrified, he sat down exactly where he was in the hallway between the bedroom doors. For more than an hour, he sat there, trying to be on guard but really just shaking and waiting for one of his parents to come home. By the time Mrs. Tandy found Mike, the sun had set and it was completely dark—both inside the house and outside

"What on earth are you doing?" his mother asked him when she saw him sitting all alone in the darkness.

Although he hadn't seen anything at all, Mike explained that he had been sure that someone or something horrible had been in the house. The thing had come close to him while he'd been reading, and he had brushed past it on the stairs.

"Do you think there's a burglar in the house?" she asked.

"No," he replied firmly. "There's someone—or something—here, but it's not a burglar. Mom, it's *totally invisible!*"

Mrs. Tandy nodded. Mike was normally honest and not easily scared. Still, it seemed that he'd freaked out for nothing because she could plainly see that nobody was in the house except for them. Mostly to make Mike feel better, but partly because it was hard to believe that her son would make up such a story, she told him, "Mike, you stay here. I'm going to get your baseball bat and we'll do a search."

With bat in hand, Michael and his mother crept slowly around the house until they'd gone from attic to basement. They found nothing at all, but somehow that didn't ease any fears. Mrs. Tandy felt extremely uncomfortable herself, although at first she couldn't have said what was causing that discomfort.

Moments later, when they heard a strange scratching noise at the front door, mother and son froze together on the staircase. Together they watched in fear as the front door opened.

It was Mr. Tandy.

As he walked through the door, he called out, "The meeting was over early and I brought some leftover doughnuts home! Let's all have a snack in the kitchen."

Michael and his mother felt pretty foolish. They slid the bat into a corner and went into the kitchen to enjoy the unexpected treat. They didn't mention the strange incidents to Mr. Tandy. For Mike, talking about the eerie experience would only have brought his horrible fear back.

Over the next few days, neither mother nor son spoke of that scary evening. Life pretty much settled back into a routine. Everything was back to normal.

Well, almost.

Mike still felt creeped out when he was in the living room, especially near the fireplace. He didn't mention it to anyone, but he tried to avoid that part of the house, especially when he was by himself. He couldn't stay away entirely because his fish tank was there in the living room. But Mike managed to check on his scaly swimmers only once a week, not daily. The rest of the time, he just worried about them. He simply couldn't bear the feeling of evil that he got when he was near the tank.

For many weeks, Michael kept all his spooky feelings to himself. Finally, he could take it no longer. He asked his mother if she had ever felt anything weird near the fireplace or the aquarium. She said no and tried to assure him that everything was all right, that he was maybe still scared from the night he'd been babysitting. Mike could tell from her tone of voice that she had decided his imagination had worked overtime that evening because there had been no adults in the house.

By the end of the following week, Mike felt that the spooky vibes had changed. Now they were not just spooky. They were filled with utter dread. But Michael didn't say anything to his parents.

As it turned out, he didn't have to.

The very next day, while Mr. Tandy and Michael were out at a soccer match, Mrs. Tandy realized that she should never have doubted Michael's word.

She was sitting in the living room looking over some papers when she began to feel strangely uncomfortable. At first, she thought there must be a draft, so she closed the window, put a sweater on and went back to work. She still felt strange, very strange indeed—and not strange in a good way.

Mrs. Tandy wondered if maybe she was hungry. She went into the kitchen and fixed herself a snack. As she walked back into the living room, she thought, *This is so weird. Usually I love being alone in the house. What's different this time? What's wrong?*

The atmosphere in the room suddenly became worse. She was sure that someone was nearby, glaring angrily at her. But when she glanced about, Mrs.

Tandy could see that the only other living things were the fish in the tank. *Odd,* she thought, *they seem to be swimming much faster than usual.*

Then she noticed something else—something that was impossible. Her plate fell to the floor, shattering into dozens of tiny pieces. She blinked her eyes and looked again. There was no mistake. The enormous fish tank was not resting on its specially built table. It was on the floor near where it had been.

Mrs. Tandy screamed. *This couldn't be happening!* The aquarium couldn't possibly have moved by itself! It took at least four strong people to even budge that tank.

The woman's scream caught the attention of half a dozen boys from the nearby school. They had been riding past on their bicycles and raced to the house to help. Mrs. Tandy was grateful for their company, but they didn't understand when she tried to explain what had happened. Nevertheless, the boys joined forces and helped Mrs. Tandy lift the fish tank back up onto the proper table. They were very careful, but some water spilled out of the aquarium and onto the living room floor.

Mrs. Tandy showed the helpful students to the door and thanked them, then returned to the living room to wipe up the spilt water.

As she soaked up the small puddles, she thought, *How could this have happened? How could the tank have moved while I was in the kitchen? How did it move at all without spilling even one dribble of water?*

Mrs. Tandy didn't have much time to think about the frightening implications of those questions because just then Michael and his father arrived back home. When they asked her why she was wiping the floor, she hesitated for a moment. Should she say anything about what had just happened? In a split second, she decided instead to mumble something about having spilled a drink.

Both Michael and his father could easily see that there was no drinking glass anywhere in the living room, but they chose not to say anything more.

From that moment on, it became hard for either Mike or his mother to deny that there was something very odd in their home. Neither said anything to the other, but both mother and son were wondering if the house was haunted. Even Mr. Tandy began to feel a cold fear whenever he went into the corner of the living room where the fish tank stood. Often, shortly after any of the three Tandys felt that fear, they would hear footsteps cross the room and begin to climb the stairs.

Over time, the haunting gained strength. Just a few days after the fish tank had mysteriously moved, mom, dad and Mike finally admitted to each other that something was wrong. They all agreed not to say anything to little Mary Beth because it would just frighten the child.

For the next few weeks, loud ghostly moans and knocks woke the family up. After they were wakened, fear kept them awake. Sometimes they also noticed terrible smells—smells that were especially strong in the living room. One day, as Michael approached the aquarium to tend to his fish, thick black clouds billowed out from the fireplace and into the rest of the house.

Mike ran to the kitchen where he told his parents about an image that had come toward him. It was a smoky image, he explained, of a "nasty old man." That was the moment when the Tandys finally accepted reality. Some sort of dreadful and unnatural force was haunting their home.

They also knew that they'd had enough. Quickly packing up what they needed for a night away, the family went to a nearby hotel. Mike was so relieved to be out of the horrible house that he did not even think about the beloved tropical fish he'd left behind.

The next morning, the Tandys agreed to ask some questions about the history of their house. What they found out did not ease their minds. Apparently, the private school that had hired Mr. Tandy had not given him the biggest house on the school grounds because they were so eager to have him as a teacher.

No, not at all.

The Tandys had been given the big house because the new teacher was the only one on staff who would agree to live in the place. The rest of the teachers and staff knew that the property had a reputation for being haunted by a very unpleasant spirit.

"I don't think we should move back in there," Mike offered. "Summer holidays are nearly here anyway. Let's stay in the hotel until we can ship all of our things back home to Ireland. I don't ever want to see that place again. It's just too spooky! I don't even want to go back in to get my fish. Someone else can do that."

Mike's parents nodded in agreement.

And so, just a few weeks later, the Tandy family, and Mike's tropical fish, were settled back into their old familiar neighborhood in Ireland. They had escaped from the invisible evil that had tried to force itself into their lives.

Or had they?

One evening, Mike was playing ball on the front lawn with some of his old friends. When it became dark, the boys all headed home and Mike went back into the house for the night. As he stepped through the doorway, he felt an unwelcome and eerily familiar sensation—some invisible something had brushed past him.

The boy stood still, his heart pounding uncomfortably in his chest. When he heard heavy footfalls just in front of him, he wondered if his poor heart would stop. Mike croaked out a terrified scream. His parents came running to the doorway where he stood.

"What's wrong, Michael?" his father asked, after glancing around the room. Neither Mr. Tandy nor his wife could see, hear or feel anything that might have made their son scream—until their eyes followed the boy's pointed finger. The aquarium had moved. The incredibly heavy tank once again rested on the floor beside its specially designed table.

Just like the last time, not a drop of water had spilled out of the tank. Worse, the fish were swimming frantically about at a speed easily three times their normal rate. The Tandys silently made their way to the living room. When they reached the doorway, a cold draft whooshed past them.

The three turned to flee from the room, but they were trapped. There, just in front of them, stood the smoky apparition of the nasty old man. The horrible ghost must somehow have attached himself to the fish tank and followed them back to Ireland. Michael's aquarium had become a haunted house for fish!

Mrs. Tandy ran and got Mary Beth then followed her husband and son past the unmoving, filmy manifestation. For nearly an hour, everyone except Mary Beth, who was too young to fear a ghost, stood on the front lawn in the dark, shaking in terror. A neighbor from across the street finally noticed the family and its distress, and he invited the Tandys into the safety of his own home for the night.

Although no one in that house slept very well either, at least they were safe until morning when they could call for help. By noon the next day, psychic investigators swarmed the Tandy house. The haunting had obviously become worse. Waves were splashing up against the sides of the fish tank, but not even one drop dribbled out.

A horrible smell filled the place. The stench became so bad that it finally forced everyone, even the psychics, away from the property. They stood on the nearby sidewalk, trembling in fear. Loud crashes and tremendous bangs echoed throughout the house—a house that was empty of all living beings, except tiny tropical fish swimming in a haunted aquarium.

Soon the commotion attracted other people's attention. No one was foolish enough to go near the place while the supernatural racket was going on. The chaos continued for hours. When it stopped, Michael's father and the neighbor from across the street slowly made their way up the front walk to the house. They pushed open the front door and fearfully walked inside.

Mr. Tandy could only whisper, "Oh, my," for he could hardly believe his eyes. The family's possessions were strewn all over the floors in every room. Heavy furniture had been smashed, and artwork had been broken into pieces. Someone or something very powerful had trashed the house and everything in it.

No one had ever seen such damage. Nothing had been left untouched. Even the family's clothes had been dumped out of drawers, ripped up and tossed around. Confusion and fear gripped the brave little group. The Tandys agreed that they couldn't possibly spend one more night in their house. Slowly the crowd began to disperse. Michael and his parents retreated to the house across the street where they'd spent the previous night.

That evening, as Michael got ready for bed, his father made a phone call to the principal of the school in England where the nightmare had begun. The principal had evidently started a thorough investigation that had included digging up patches of the lawn around the house where the Tandys had tried to live. The principal thought that he had tracked down the source of the haunting.

It seems that a pile of bones—human bones estimated to be nearly 200 years old—had been found buried near the living room window. No one connected with the school, or even the town, had any idea whose bones they were or how they came to be buried there. Each bone was so old and dry that it crumbled almost to dust when it was lifted from its resting place. Could this have been the skeleton of the nasty old ghost?

It's unlikely that anyone will ever know the answer to that question.

We do know that the next day, when the Tandys got up the nerve to go inside the house to check on the aquarium, they found the atmosphere in the house quite different—lighter, somehow. There was still a mess to be cleaned up, but the place just seemed more peaceful.

That afternoon, the psychics came back and quietly walked through the house. They confirmed what the Tandys had already suspected. The ghost was gone.

The Tandy family had survived their terrible supernatural ordeal. Sadly, Michael's fish had not. The aquarium had been smashed into thousands of jagged fragments and every fish was dead.

A FAITHFUL
COMPANION

Elizabeth Morgan lived with her parents in the south of England. Elizabeth was a bright little girl and happy most of the time but just before her fourth birthday there were times when her parents thought that she seemed especially quiet.

Elizabeth's father wondered if the child was lonely. He suggested buying a pet. "A dog would keep Elizabeth company," he told his wife, "at least until she starts kindergarten and has a chance to meet some playmates."

Elizabeth's mother nodded and agreed that they would buy a dog for a birthday present for their child. Elizabeth of course knew nothing of her parents' plan and her quiet, solitary life continued right up until the evening before her fourth birthday.

The first unusual thing about that evening was that Elizabeth's father wasn't home for supper. Elizabeth asked her mother about this strange situation but didn't really get a proper answer. A few hours later, when bedtime rolled around and Elizabeth's father was still not home, the little girl became angry.

"Why isn't Dad here to put me to bed?" she asked.

"I told you at supper, he had some late business to attend to. He'll be along soon, I'm sure."

Although Elizabeth was not even a little bit pleased—with her father's absence or with her mother's explanation—she fell asleep with pleasant visions of tomorrow's party dress, birthday cake and visits from grandparents.

In the morning, as always, Elizabeth woke up just before her parents came into her room to wake her up. She never told them that she was awake in the morning before they came into her room. Instead, she always let them think that their kisses had wakened her. This morning, the morning of her birthday, she was especially delighted with the few moments of being alone and awake. She hugged herself with joy. *It's my birthday. I'm four!* Elizabeth thought.

A few minutes later, her bedroom door opened and she heard the familiar sounds of her parents' slippers moving across the floor. Despite her excitement about this special day, Elizabeth managed to keep her eyes closed, pretending to be asleep as her mother and father approached her bed.

That day, however, she didn't get her usual wake-up kiss. Instead, something small and damp dragged across the side of her face. Elizabeth opened her eyes in a flash, and her hand flew up to wipe her wet cheek. Then she saw him. There, on her bed, was a tiny golden bundle of fur with big paws and floppy ears, wagging its tail and wriggling and tugging at the bedclothes.

"A puppy!" Elizabeth exclaimed, excitedly patting the small dog. "He's the cutest thing I've ever seen. Who does he belong to?"

"Happy Birthday, Elizabeth," her parents chimed together. His father continued, "His name is Laddie and he's your dog. He's our birthday present to you. The reason I was late getting home yesterday was because I was picking him up."

"He's mine? He's really mine?" the little girl asked over and over again.

During the day, Elizabeth tried to be polite to all the people who came to the house to help celebrate her birthday, but all she really wanted to do was play with Laddie.

From that day on, Laddie and Elizabeth were almost always together. The dog stayed in the backyard when the little girl played on her swings or in her sandbox. When Elizabeth and her mother went for walks, they put Laddie's leash on and the dog went too. Her parents were delighted to see that the signs of loneliness they'd worried about were gone completely.

A year later, Elizabeth's fifth birthday was not nearly as thrilling an event as her fourth birthday had been, but it did bring its own excitement, since she would soon be starting school. On the first morning, Elizabeth, her mother and Laddie walked to the school.

"Laddie and I will be right here on the sidewalk when you come out," her mother told Elizabeth as they entered the schoolyard.

"Okay, Mom. I'll be fine. Bye now. I have to go."

Elizabeth kissed her mother and petted Laddie before skipping happily into the school. At the end of the school day, as promised, her mother and Laddie were waiting to walk her home.

After a few weeks of this routine, Elizabeth's mother stopped walking right up to the school gate. When they were a block away from the school, her mother told her, "Laddie and I are going to stop here, Elizabeth, and we'll be waiting here when you head for home."

"I'll be fine, Mom," the little girl once again assured her mother. Secretly, Elizabeth was pleased with the extra independence and, by the end of the school year, she was walking by herself all the way back and forth between home and school.

The child's mother always knew when it was time for Elizabeth's arrival home because Laddie would begin fussing and whining and scratching at the door. The dog wanted to be let out into the front yard so he could always be the first to greet his favorite person.

This routine went on for years, right up until Elizabeth's eighth birthday, when just one little thing changed. Her parents bought a piano and arranged for Elizabeth to take lessons from a neighbor. Now, on Thursdays after school she went to her music teacher's house. Laddie soon learned that routine, too, and always begged to be let out a second time just before his companion was about to come home.

The years passed. Elizabeth enjoyed playing the piano; she had fun at school and made lots of friends. Laddie, however, was still her very best friend.

One afternoon, when she was 11, Elizabeth was surprised to notice that Laddie was not waiting for her after school. *Something is wrong,* she thought as she checked the yard in case he was hiding in the bushes. Her heart pounded hard in her chest. Frozen with fear, the girl could do nothing but scream for her mother. The front door flew open and Elizabeth's mother came running down the porch steps. She hugged her daughter close.

"It's Laddie, Elizabeth. He's not well. Dad's coming home from work. We need to take the dog to the veterinarian's office."

Elizabeth slowly walked into the house. Blankets and newspapers and bowls of water and food were strewn all over the floor. In the middle of the clutter lay Laddie. He looked so sick that at first Elizabeth thought he was dead. Then he opened one eye. When Laddie saw that it was his girl approaching, he found the energy to greet her with two thumps of his tail against the floor.

Elizabeth picked the suffering animal up and held him until her father came home. Together, the family took their beloved pet for his last-ever car ride.

"It's hopeless," the vet told them. "He's too sick. I can't save him. The kindest thing to do is put him out of his misery."

Elizabeth, her mother and her father nodded their agreement. It was time to let Laddie go.

For the next few days, the family home just wasn't the same. It was much quieter. Rooms seemed bigger and emptier. There was very little talk and even less laughter in the house. Elizabeth stayed home from school until after the weekend. By Monday, however, she realized that she just couldn't cry any more.

Once Elizabeth was back on the school grounds and playing with her friends, she could almost forget how sad she felt. Inside the classroom, it was even easier because she had to try hard to learn her lessons.

The most difficult part came at the end of that school day. Elizabeth knew that Laddie would not be waiting for her to come home from school. As she made her way home, the sad girl walked more and more slowly. By the time she approached the gate to her front yard, she was barely moving. She wondered if she had the courage to open the gate and walk alone among the huge, old trees up to the house.

Determined to be brave, Elizabeth took a deep breath, put her hand on the gate and pushed it open. She didn't get far, for right before her eyes was a dog. *How could that be?* she wondered. *I know he's dead.* But this animal was wagging his tail excitedly just as Laddie always had. *He even acts like Laddie,* she thought.

At first, Elizabeth stood frozen with fear. Slowly she knelt down to pet the dog, but the animal scampered away and stayed just out of Elizabeth's reach.

"Come here, boy, it's me, Elizabeth. Come here and let me pet you," she coached, but the dog would not approach her. Instead, this mysterious animal, who seemed to be Laddie but couldn't possibly have been Laddie, just ran back and forth across the yard. The dog was clearly very happy to see his girl but no matter how much she coaxed he would not come to her side, nor would he allow her to come to him.

The two best friends played like this for a few minutes until Elizabeth's mother opened the front door and called to her daughter to come inside.

Should I tell her that Laddie's back? Elizabeth wondered. Before she had a chance to say anything, the

dog vanished completely. Confused, the girl followed her mother into the house. They sat together in the kitchen for a while, but Elizabeth couldn't find a good time to tell her mother about the strange experience she'd just had.

That night, as the child lay in her bed, she finally figured out what had happened to her earlier in her front yard.

I saw a ghost. I really and truly saw a ghost. Not just any ghost. I saw Laddie's ghost.

The next morning, Elizabeth was anxious to get out the door to see if the phantom dog was back. He wasn't.

I guess he's gone for good now, she decided, but as she reached the front gate, Elizabeth was sure she heard a noise that sounded like a dog panting. "Laddie?" she called. There was no response. Disappointed, she closed the gate and walked to school.

That day, Elizabeth walked home with two girl-friends. The three had been chatting happily and so, when she arrived at the entrance to her own yard, Elizabeth wasn't thinking about Laddie or his ghost. She waved goodbye to her friends before opening the gate. As soon as she stepped foot inside the yard, however, she saw Laddie—or at least his spirit. There he was, as full of energy and as happy to see her as he'd always been.

"Laddie, Laddie, come here," she said to the dog's ghost but, once again, the ghostly animal would not come to her. The phantom dog just ran about, wagging his tail, until Elizabeth reached the front door. Then the ghostly animal vanished.

I can't tell Mom or Dad that I've seen Laddie's ghost. They'll think I'm crazy. Besides, it might spoil the magic and he might never come back to see me again, she thought. Elizabeth enjoyed her ghost pet's brief visits far too much to risk having that happen.

As autumn became winter, Elizabeth counted on seeing the dog's apparition every day after school. When her parents offered to get her another dog, she said no, afraid that a living animal would frighten Laddie's ghost away.

Her loyalty to the dog's spirit soon paid off for Elizabeth. Late in November, her classroom teacher asked her to stay after school to play the piano for the choir's Christmas concert rehearsal. It was dark by the time the girl left. She hurried home as quickly as she could, knowing that her mother would be concerned.

Just as she rounded the last corner on the route home, two boys jumped out from behind some bushes. They stood right in front of the girl, blocking her path. Both of them were bigger than she was. They meant trouble, Elizabeth knew.

"What do you want?" the frightened girl asked.

"We want to bug you," one of the boys replied.

"Why?" she asked. "You don't even know me. I've never done anything to you."

"We don't care," said the other boy, shoving his palm against her shoulder.

"Stop it. That hurt," Elizabeth said as she slowly inched her way backward, hoping to get away from the bullies.

"It was supposed to hurt," the boy sneered, but he barely had time to get those words out of his mouth before a growling, golden dog appeared from nowhere and charged at the boy. The dog's lips were pulled back in a snarl. It leapt first at one boy and then at the other. It was clear to the bullies that the dog was very angry and was going to attack someone. The boys pushed past Elizabeth so hard and fast that they knocked her over. She didn't know for sure if she was hurt, but at least they were gone.

"Laddie," the girl called to the dog's image. "Thank you. You saved me. Come here, Laddie. Let me pet you."

But the dog had already vanished. Shaken by the run-in with those horrible boys, Elizabeth ran the rest of the way home. When she got to her yard, there was Laddie—or his ghost.

The following Thursday afternoon, as Elizabeth set out for her weekly piano lesson, her father said, "It'll be dark out by the time you get back, so I'll meet you at the gate. We can walk across the yard together."

"That's okay, Dad. You don't have to do that. Laddie's always there for me," Elizabeth said before pausing. "Oh my goodness, I didn't mean to say that. I've told you my secret, haven't I?"

Her father simply stared at her.

"Dad, he's there for me every day, when I come home from school or music lessons. I guess it couldn't really be Laddie anymore. It must be his ghost." Elizabeth said.

"How long has this been going on?" her father asked in a strange tone of voice.

"For years, Dad. It's nothing to worry about," the girl assured her father.

"Why didn't you tell us?"

"I guess because it was one of those secrets that I wanted to keep to myself and, besides, I didn't know if you or Mom would believe me."

Elizabeth's father was quiet for a long time before he finally spoke. "I believe you, Elizabeth. I believe that Laddie's ghost has been here almost since the day he died. I believe you because I see him, too."

Laddie's ghost continued to appear to both Elizabeth and her father all through her school years. Elizabeth never knew whether her mother ever saw the dog's ghost or not. Maybe that was one of those secrets that some adults like to keep to themselves.

ROOMMATES

When Kris Maher was in her early twenties, she rented an apartment on West 46th Street in New York City. She was delighted with her new place, which was also close to her job and to all her friends.

Kris settled into the apartment easily. Looking around the rooms, she imagined living there forever. Kris liked her new place so much that she began staying up late simply to enjoy being in her new home a little longer.

Over the following few months, however, Kris occasionally noticed something a bit odd. There seemed to be a small, blurry spot in her vision every now and then. At first she wondered if it meant she wasn't getting enough sleep, so she started going to bed a little earlier. That seemed to help, because she didn't see the blurry patch nearly as often.

One Saturday morning, after a good night's sleep, Kris was walking from her bedroom into the kitchen when the blur appeared again. Not everything was blurred—just one little spot. It was as though a mist or a fog had scuttled across the floor. Just a second later, the blur vanished. Kris was upset, partly because she didn't want to think she might be developing an eye problem, and partly because she didn't want to think she was seeing things. The confused young woman sat down on the living room couch. The misty motion had been so real and so sudden. She needed a moment to sit still and think.

A few minutes later, Kris got up and made some breakfast, then headed out to meet some friends. Several hours later, she arrived back at her apartment in a great mood and ready for a shower. As she walked through the living room toward the bathroom, something caught Kris's eye again. This time it wasn't anything like the small, low-lying fog that had upset her earlier in the day. This time it was quite different, but she really couldn't figure out how. She decided to ignore whatever it was and went into the bathroom.

Once there, Kris reached into the bathtub and turned on the taps. Moments later, with warm water pouring from the showerhead, Kris stepped into the bathtub.

Suddenly she let out a loud squeal, jumped out of the tub, whirled around and looked down. There, on the bottom of the bathtub, lay her cotton place mats—the ones that belonged on her dining room table.

How on earth could my place mats get into the bathtub? Kris thought while backing out of the bathroom toward the dining room. She glanced over at the table and saw that the tabletop was bare.

Kris stumbled into the kitchen. Everything there was in its place. She moved into her bedroom. *Nothing odd here,* she noted with relief.

The usually calm woman began to feel rather foolish. She went back into the bathroom, took the place mats out of the tub and put them in the sink to dry, while trying to push the bizarre incident out of her mind. Then she got back into the shower and finished it without any surprises.

The next morning, Kris awoke feeling refreshed. As she sat up at the edge of the bed, she began to remember a snippet of a dream she'd had. She couldn't recall

all of the details of the dream—and in fact she couldn't even be sure that it was a dream.

But it must have been. What else could explain her strange memory of a small white cat curled up beside her as she slept?

Definitely weird, she thought, *I haven't had an imaginary pet since I was a little kid. Well at least I got a good sleep.*

Over the next few weeks, Kris became accustomed to feeling that a cat was sleeping next to her. Every night, shortly after she went to sleep, Kris would dream that a cat jumped up onto her bed. The "imaginary" little animal always pumped its paws a few times on the blanket and then settled down to sleep with her. Before long, Kris looked forward to the visits from her invisible friend. After all, she could enjoy the companionship of a pet with none of the work or responsibility that came with a real one. Kris soon became as pleased with her part-time pet as she was with her apartment.

One Monday morning when she was rushing to get ready for work, Kris thought she saw something small and white in a corner of the dining room, but she was in such a hurry to catch her bus that she didn't pay much attention to the sight. It wasn't until she sat down in her office that she realized what it was she'd seen in that brief instant before running out of the apartment.

That was a cat I saw, she thought. *It was a white cat. I'm sure it was. How silly! Why do I have cats on my mind these days?* Kris wondered.

At lunch Kris told one of her friends about the strange experiences in her apartment. She talked about the quick-moving fog by the floor and about the place mats in the bathtub. Then she described the feeling that a cat was sleeping with her and that she'd seen a cat in her apartment earlier that day. Her friend suggested that Kris was lonely and maybe needed a real pet for company.

Kris knew that taking on the responsibility for an animal was a serious matter. She'd have to make the decision very carefully—not when she was feeling rattled from the mysterious goings-on in her apartment.

After a few more nights of dreaming about a cat sleeping beside her, Kris began to see the animal regularly—even when she was wide awake. The first time actually scared her, and each time it happened she paced around the apartment wondering, *Am I losing my mind? Am I seeing a ghost?* Both thoughts worried her. She decided to take a day off work. *I'm letting that spooky white formation completely upset me,* she realized with a bit of embarrassment.

The next day, she sat up in her bed and said out loud—to an empty apartment—"I do want a pet! I'm going to get a kitten. Today!"

If Kris had thought her apartment was empty, apparently it wasn't. As she walked toward the front door, she was sure she heard something tiny racing across the dining room floor.

Kris laughed. *I was right. My mind really does want me to get a cat. Now I'm even hearing the patter of little claws on wood floors.*

She was going to buy a kitten! *I'll name him Tiger and he'll be my furry roommate. Then I'll stop seeing and feeling such weird things because I won't be lonely anymore.*

The moment Kris approached the pet-shop window, she saw her new pet. Curled up in the corner of a display case was the cutest tabby kitten she had ever seen. Inside the store, the shop clerk lifted the tabby ball of fluff from his display case and handed him to Kris. The kitten mewed loudly. Kris took him from the shop owner.

"This is Tiger," she told the man as she fumbled for her wallet.

Kris didn't put Tiger down again until the two of them were back inside her apartment. She thought the little cat might be exhausted from all the excitement of being adopted, so she took him into the bedroom and put him on the pillow for a nap.

A short time later, Kris couldn't wait any longer to play with Tiger, so she carried him into the living room and sat down on the couch. The kitten lay quietly on her lap and looked around his new home. *This is just perfect,* Kris thought.

Suddenly, Tiger jumped to his feet. His tiny, sharp claws scratched Kris's legs as he bolted up and fled—from something. But from what? What had startled the animal? And where on earth did he go? Kris couldn't see him anywhere.

More than a bit puzzled and frightened, Kris forced herself to walk slowly and quietly around the room. The loudest noise she could hear was the beating of her own heart. Otherwise she didn't hear or see anything out of the ordinary. Then she heard the distinctive sounds of a cat fight by her door.

She looked down the hall. There was Tiger, looking as if he was fighting for his life.

But fighting with what? Kris wondered, almost in a panic. She bent down to pick up the feisty kitten.

Suddenly, something clawed at Kris's hand—not Tiger, but something invisible between her and her new kitty. She grabbed the tiny tabby and ran to the bedroom, slamming the door closed behind her.

Kris could feel Tiger's heart pounding as hard and fast as her own. She sat on the bed with the kitten in her lap until they both began to calm down.

"Is there something wrong with you?" she asked her new kitten. "What happened out there? Did you just have a seizure? Are you sick? What should I be doing for you, poor thing?"

Of course, a six-week old cat couldn't solve the problem. Not knowing what else to do, Kris phoned the pet shop.

"Could there be something wrong with the kitten that I just bought from you?" she asked.

"I doubt it, ma'am. The vet just checked him over yesterday. What's the matter with him?" the owner replied.

Kris explained that Tiger seemed to have been in a struggle for his life against something only the cat could see.

"It was so bad that even I got scratched," she added.

"Has anything unusual happened in your apartment before this?" the man probed.

Kris hesitated. Should she tell the pet-shop owner that the only disturbances were directly connected with the reason she adopted Tiger? That she seemed to be so lonely she was imagining that a cat was already in the apartment sleeping in her bed at night? That she thought she might be losing her mind?

When she didn't immediately reply, the man continued, "Did you say you live on West 46th?"

"Yes," Kris replied, somewhat hesitantly.

"In one of those old apartment buildings?" he asked.

"Yes. Why?"

"Well," the pet shop owner began slowly. "I've heard this sort of thing before." He paused. "You know, those buildings used to be warehouses, and the owners kept cats to help keep out the mice and rats. Those cats were really dedicated to guarding their territories—and apparently some of them have never left. Their spirits came back after death to haunt their old homes."

Kris was speechless. If the shop owner was right, she was living in a haunted apartment. A shudder ran from the top of Kris's head down to the soles of her feet.

The man continued, "I'm sure you'll be glad to know that most times the ghost cat and the living cat do eventually learn to get along with one another. It could take some time, though."

Before she put down the phone, Kris stammered, "Thank you. I'll let you know what happens."

My apartment's haunted, Kris thought over and over again as she picked up Tiger and held him close. She looked down at the tiny animal purring contentedly in her arms. *I wanted a cat, but now I have two! I have a real cat and a phantom cat. Worse, they don't get along!*

Kris thought for a while longer about what she should do next. Finally she made up her mind. Tiger had fallen asleep in her arms, so she put him down gently on her pillow. "You stay right here while I try to make this better for all of us."

Closing the bedroom door behind her, Kris searched the rest of her apartment for the invisible pet. One of the problems with having ghost cat is that you don't always know where it is. So Kris poured a bit of milk into a saucer and put it down in the corner of the dining room where she'd seen the white mist. Then she sat down beside it. Feeling extremely foolish, she began to speak very softly and quietly. She was unsure whether the phantom cat was able to understand her words of comfort or, more likely, its soul was just comforted by the soothing sound of her voice.

"I'm going to give you a name. Spook. Your name is Spook and if you're going to haunt this apartment, my spooky little friend, you have to stop picking on Tiger. He's just a little kitten. You could hurt him."

She could not see or hear any movement in the apartment but a few seconds later she felt something soft rub gently up against her leg.

"Thank you, Spook," she said.

Over the next few years, Kris became very used to living with her two cats—one from this life, one from the afterlife. Sometimes she would see Tiger tearing around the apartment as though he was chasing something. Other times, something seemed to be chasing him. Sometimes Tiger would stick out his tongue as though he was cleaning something. Other times he would lie on the couch purring, moving his head around as if he was being licked by something Kris couldn't see.

Every now and then, from the corner of her eye, Kris could see the outline of her ghost kitty. And every night when she went to bed, Kris could count on having two cats snuggle up against her, purring happily until all three roommates fell asleep.

MOUNTAIN PHANTOMS

Kyle always looked forward to the first weekend of summer, not just because it meant the end of school and the beginning of summer holidays, but also because it was the one weekend in the entire year that his Uncle Dave came to visit. The man traveled all over the world and always had exciting adventures to tell. Like the time he'd been in a small village nestled in a valley…

"It was a strange little place, this one," Uncle Dave began. "Some of the women in the village were old. I mean really old. They were over a hundred years old! That was weird enough, but the stories they told were even creepier. The worst one, for my friends and me, was about the ancient evil phantoms—supernatural beasts that lived in the caves and crevices of the mountains that surrounded their town."

These wrinkly, wretched-looking old crones warned that if anyone tried to climb the nearby mountain slopes, the climbers' lives would be in deadly peril. "Wicked and unnatural birds live up there," one toothless old hag confided.

Of course, Kyle's uncle and his friends knew that the women's tales must just be legends, folklore from hundreds of years before. "There can't be any truth to the stories," Dave told his friends. "These women are so old that their minds have shriveled. Besides, even when they were young and healthy they still were simple, uneducated peasants. They probably never realized that there are no such thing as 'spirits,' especially not the spirits of birds!"

One of Dave's friends suggested that they should hike up the mountainside the very next day. "Then," he explained, "when we get back to town in the evening, we can prove to these frightened people that there is nothing 'unnatural' at all near their homes."

The hair rose on the back of Kyle's neck, and he tingled with excitement and fear as he listened to Uncle Dave's words. The boy almost wanted to shout "Don't!" even though he knew the eerie adventure had happened months before. And, for just for the briefest of moments, Kyle wondered if maybe Dave and his friends were more foolhardy than brave.

Early the next morning, the group of friends prepared for their trek without a worry in the world. No crazy old ladies' superstitions could harm them—especially not on such a beautiful, sunny day. At least that's what the climbers thought.

And, perhaps if they'd heeded the wise old sages' warning, nothing frightening would have happened that day. "It's good that we're here to show these simple people there is nothing to fear," Dave told his friends confidently at the outset. They chatted and joked among themselves as they climbed the steep slope.

All went well for the better part of an hour.

Then, everything changed—instantly, drastically and dangerously.

In the blink of an eye, the sunshine and clear blue sky went dark. Thunderous sounds bellowed from the blackened sky. Fearfully, the adventurers looked toward the mountaintops, but all they could see was an enormous flock of huge, ugly birds circling above them. Hundreds of gargantuan, jagged wings flapped deafeningly, drowning out all other sounds.

With sharp, piercing black eyes, the flying creatures stared down menacingly at the human intruders. Frozen in terror, the group was assaulted by the birds' vile and unnatural display of hate. No one dared to move, but their stillness enraged the birds even more. The huge, flying beasts began squawking and cawing.

"Head back down!" Kyle's uncle screamed to his friends as he scrambled down the hillside. The ferocious birds swooped down to attack them. In their haste to escape, first one climber, and then the others, tumbled head over heels down the craggy mountainside, banging and scraping themselves against the rocks.

The instant they were at the bottom of the slope, the sun suddenly shone brightly again and the sky was clear. Every one of the hundreds of vicious birds had vanished as quickly and mysteriously as they had appeared. It was like magic—a bizarre and evil kind of magic.

"I'll tell you, Kyle," Uncle Dave continued, "none of us has been the same since. Our cuts and bruises eventually healed, but the terror, that terror of being threatened by hundreds of ghastly swarming birds, has never been far from our minds."

In a shivery whisper of a voice, Dave acknowledged that the adventurers were so tormented by the memory of their experience that, months later, they decided to investigate the types of birds they'd seen flying above them on that awful morning. They wanted very badly to prove to themselves that the ugly creatures were simply a species of hostile mountain-dwelling birds.

Sadly, their plan to ease their minds did not work.

"An ornithologist, that's an expert on birds," Uncle Dave explained, "told us that such winged creatures did not exist—at least not now, not in this world. They haven't existed for thousands of years. He said these were *rocs*—prehistoric predators from the time of the dinosaurs. Like the dinosaurs, these flying creatures have been extinct for millions and millions of years. It seemed that those crazy old women weren't so crazy after all. Somehow they knew about those ancient, angry ghosts."

Kyle shrugged his shoulders to loosen the muscles that had tensed while he'd been listening to his hero's encounter with the supernatural. After he'd taken a deep breath, Uncle Dave continued to talk, but more to himself than to Kyle, it seemed.

"What are these beasts? Some say they are the ghosts of rocs. Others believe that they're specters of people, thieves whose dishonest souls will forever haunt the places where their stolen treasures are hidden."

By the time Uncle Dave had finished telling of his encounter with the bizarre specters of doom, it was well after midnight and Kyle was so tired that he could barely climb the stairs to his bedroom. Even so, it took a long time for him to fall asleep.

THE CAT AND THE TIES

Most ghost stories are at least a little bit frightening. Not very many of them are silly, but this one definitely is.

Joseph Farini hated animals, especially cats. Now that would have been fine except that his wife, Angelina Farini, loved animals, especially cats.

One day, on her way home from work, Mrs. Farini heard a faint mewing sound coming from beside a building. Then she saw the saddest-looking stray kitten anyone had ever seen—a little orange puff of mewing fur. His eyes and ears looked too big for the kitty head they were attached to.

The woman couldn't leave the pathetic creature to die on the sidewalk, so she picked him up. On the walk home, Angelina decided that she was going to keep the tiny tabby, even though she knew that bringing him home was going to cause problems. Not only would Joseph object, but their apartment building did not allow pets.

Angelina named the kitten Boomer. Within just a few days, Boomer became very spoiled. Angelina allowed him to take his morning catnaps in Joseph's favorite chair—even on Saturdays when Joseph himself wanted to nap in that chair. Angelina also allowed the cat to sit on the kitchen table at mealtimes. Joseph was not impressed.

Worse, Boomer didn't like Joseph any better than Joseph liked Boomer! By the end of their first week together, it was clear that a battle between man and kitten had begun. Joseph was never exactly mean to the cat, but he was never kind to him either. Boomer soon found his own way to show his feelings toward Joseph. Good grooming and dressing well were very important to Mr. Farini. He rarely wore anything other than a suit and tie. He was fussy about all of his clothes, and extra fussy about his ties.

The clever little Boomer must have been able to sense Joseph's fussiness because the cat regularly pawed his way into the bedroom closet and pulled down as many of Joseph's ties as he could reach. Once Boomer had a tie down on the floor, at a comfortable kitty-level, he would shred it to bits with his sharp claws. Within a month, Joseph had only one tie left and absolutely no patience for the cat.

When the landlord discovered that the Farinis had a pet, he told them they could either move or give up the cat. Of course, Joseph voted to get rid of Boomer. After much thought and many hours of sadness, Angelina decided she would have to take the cat to her parents' farm.

Unfortunately, Boomer hated being a farm cat. He knew nothing about the dangers of farm equipment and so was always getting in the way of the tractors and the combines. Late at night on the second Sunday that Boomer was at the farm, the cat managed to get in the way for the very last time. Poor Boomer was run over by a tractor.

The night of the accident, Angelina was away on business and Joseph was asleep in bed. Just before midnight, a strange noise awakened him from his slumber. At first Joseph thought the noise was coming from far away, but after listening for a while, he wondered if the mysterious sounds were coming from someplace very close—perhaps even his own bedroom.

For some reason that he could never explain, Joseph felt just a bit afraid. He didn't know exactly what he was afraid of, because he knew for certain that no sound, no matter how irritating it might be, could hurt him in any way. But he was too tired to care and the troubling sounds faded into the background of his mind. Not long after that, Joseph took a deep breath, rolled over and went back to sleep.

When he woke up the next morning, Joseph remembered the disturbance the night before, but he didn't give the puzzling incident much more thought. As always, while he showered and ate breakfast, Joseph decided what he was going to wear to work that day. His choices were limited because that miserable Boomer had only left him one tie. *At least that blasted animal will never destroy anything else in my closet,* Joseph thought with a smile on his face. It would now be safe for him to do some shopping and start to replace the ties that Boomer had ruined.

Oddly, of all the ties the cat had destroyed, Boomer had never gone near one particular tie. It was a tie Joseph had never liked. It was an ugly green color with an even uglier pattern on it. It was also just a little too short. Joseph had not chosen the tie for himself. His in-laws had given it to him one Christmas, and he'd always suspected that they'd bought it in the kids' department to save money. Today, however, it would have to suffice. He hastily threw it around his neck and tied it in a knot. Once he finished dressing, Joseph happily made his way to work.

By mid-morning, Joseph Farini felt that the office had become uncomfortably warm and he took off his jacket. A co-worker looked at Joseph and asked, "What happened to your tie? It's all torn and frayed at the bottom."

You guessed it.

Through the night, the night on which Boomer had been killed, the cat's spirit had somehow paused to get into the Farini's closet and damage Joseph's one remaining tie.

From that moment on, Joseph who had never before believed in anything supernatural, changed his mind. He now knew for certain there was such a thing as ghosts.

But he never did like cats very much!

A MENAGERIE

TOGETHER AGAIN

This next ghost story was told to me by a friend in California. It is an extraordinary tale in which bonds of love seem to overcome death.

Dallas has always had dogs in her life. To her, the animals are more than just pets. They are beloved companions that have been with her through good times and bad. Unfortunately, Dallas lives in an area where a deadly poison called cyanide sometimes seeps into the groundwater. It does not pose a danger to humans (because people don't usually drink out of mud puddles!), but the poisoned water has killed many animals over the years.

On April 14, 1995, Dallas found her two beautiful Malamute dogs, Elijah Lee and Micah James, dead— killed by the cyanide. Dallas was devastated by the dogs' deaths. She wrote and told me, "I've never grieved so hard in my life. I was still grieving a year later."

Poor Dallas might still be grieving today had it not been for a strange but happy coincidence. Her neighbor had some puppies, and knowing that Dallas was still missing Elijah Lee and Micah James so very much, they offered one of the pups to Dallas. She accepted their kind offer immediately and decided to call her new pet Shiloh.

"When I first laid eyes on Shiloh, she was six weeks old and had been abandoned along with her four sisters," Dallas wrote. No one knew what had happened to the mother dog, but her neighbor had found the pups and brought them home.

Of course, only a hard-hearted person could turn away from such a needy animal, but for Dallas there was something else. "I looked into Shiloh's eyes and said, 'Elijah! Elijah Lee!' It was instant recognition and my grieving ceased the moment I brought Shiloh home."

Once the dog and her new owner were home and happily settled in, Dallas began to notice unusual things. As the dog grew, Dallas saw more and more of Elijah's characteristics in Shiloh. She was soon convinced that this new dog was actually Elijah, only in "a smaller, sweeter package, so to speak."

Dallas puzzled over this. "I got to thinking, if this was Elijah who had come back to me, then Micah would follow, because those two dogs were always together. In fact, they are buried in the same grave in my pet cemetery."

Dallas continued, "It took a while, but Micah arrived back in April 2002."

Dallas named this "new" dog Lily Claire, but at the same time she also recognized the pup. "She not only looks like Micah James but her traits are identical, too. And, Lily and Shiloh are as inseparable as Micah and Elijah were."

The happy dog owner ended her letter with some interesting thoughts. "How's that for a story of reincarnation? The bottom line is that, for a second time, my 'babies' found me and each other. Our golden bond of love was so strong that not even death could keep us apart."

CHICKEN?

Most people are pretty chicken when it comes to the thought of seeing a ghost—but how would you feel if you saw the ghost of a chicken?

In Washington, D.C., the Capitol Building is rumored to be haunted by the ghosts of chickens! People who work there say they hear lots of strange sounds in the hallways. A man named William Miller, who worked in the building many years ago, claimed these were not the sounds that other workers might make, but "infernal clucking sounds."

Now, that's pretty strange, but stranger still is that it seems Mr. Miller was correct. Apparently, about 200 years ago, a man used to bring his chickens with him when he had to work in that building. It sounds as though the ghosts of those chickens are still clucking away into eternity. Some people have even seen the spirits of these birds strutting about the halls. Could be that they're still looking for more chicken feed?

Maybe you don't need to be afraid of chicken ghosts, but if you are ever in the Capitol Building in Washington, D.C., and you hear phantom clucking sounds, it might be safer to be a little bit chicken yourself!

GHOST OF A BLACK DOG?

Ghost lore is full of legends about phantom black dogs. All the stories are quite different from one another, except that I've never come across a pleasant story about such a sighting. Patricia Bick's experience when she was a child in Ireland is certainly no exception.

Patricia was born in a huge and very haunted home. She remembered that anyone who tried to walk up the driveway from the gate to the house would be stopped by the image of a black dog sitting in wait. Any visitors who came on horseback would have to dismount or their animals would rear up in fear of the supernatural guard dog and throw the rider to the ground.

A moment later, the black animal's manifestation would stand up and walk through a closed window into a nearby garden shed. Although no one ever knew for certain, most people who knew the history of the place were sure that the frightening illusion was actually not a dog at all, but the ghost of a man who, years before, had died a very tragic death at that exact spot.

PET CEMETERY

We usually think that graveyards are full of restless ghosts and spirits. It seems that the Hinsdale Animal Cemetery in Illinois is no exception. Apparently drivers have seen animal-like shapes and forms in their car's headlights as they drive past the burial ground. Anyone who has ever stopped to see the animals has been disappointed, for the phantom dog or cat disappears whenever anyone comes close.

D.C.'S D.C.

In this ghost story, the person involved did not want his real name being used, so we are going to call him John.

John worked as an overnight security guard in the well-haunted Capitol Building in Washington, D.C. We do not know whether John ever saw any of the other phantoms floating around that building, but we do know that he had a very scary ghostly encounter with the legendary Demon Cat (D.C.).

One cold January evening, John was guarding a particular section of the dark corridors that wind their way throughout the massive building. As he patrolled the hallway, he turned a corner—and stopped dead in his tracks. There seemed to be a cat just a few feet in front of him. The guard could hardly believe his eyes and strained to see the stray animal more clearly.

John assumed that he would simply pick up the visitor and carry it outside so it could wander off.

And that is what he set out to do.

But as he made his way toward the cat, John thought that it seemed to be getting bigger and bigger.

Well, I guess it's only reasonable that it would look bigger the closer I get to it, he thought, but a few seconds later John's matter-of-fact attitude was gone—driven away by cold fear.

This cat actually was getting bigger—and bigger and bigger—with every passing second.

"It was swelling," he recalls.

Paralyzed with fear, the terrified security guard tried to run away, but his feet wouldn't move. John's blood ran cold as the black cat, now the size of a tiger, moved directly toward him. The beast's cat-like purring had become a menacing growl. Its luminous eyes glowed with piercing brilliance as it drew closer and closer to John, who still couldn't move.

The animal held the man's gaze for a moment. Then, with one mighty lunge, it hurled itself at John, who felt the air move around him as the animal leaped. Sure he was going to die instantly, the man collapsed onto the cold, hard hallway.

We'll likely never know whether John fainted or knocked himself unconscious when his head hit the floor. We do know that when he regained consciousness, he was cold and clammy and his heart was racing. But he was not injured. There was not one bite or one scratch anywhere on John's body.

How could that be? How could anyone walk away from an attack by an angry, tiger-sized cat? Under ordinary circumstances, it would be impossible, but in this case there is an explanation.

The evil entity that jumped at John was not a living being. It was a well-known phantom—a harbinger, it's called. The District of Columbia's Demon Cat, as it is known, is said to appear in the hallways of the Capitol Building before a new president takes office.

John's experience took place in January, which is the month when newly elected presidents are sworn in. Let's hope that's why the unearthly beast appeared on that winter's night, because legend has it that the only other time the Demon Cat appears is before a terrible national tragedy.

WALTER THE MULE

As far back as 11-year-old Jamal could remember, his neighbor, Miss Wilson, had been old. The woman had a wrinkly face and barely any teeth left in her head. She had a pointed chin and scraggly grayish hair. When she walked she was all stooped over and moved ever so slowly.

Jamal knew that Miss Wilson had lived all her life in their small, quiet village. He was pretty sure that no one ever went to visit Miss Wilson. Jamal knew that when he collected the money from his paper route customers the old woman was the only one who never said anything to him. She just handed him a few crumpled bills and some change and then closed the wooden door to her run-down old cottage.

Everyone in the village pretty much left their strange old neighbor alone. Perhaps they felt uncomfortable with her odd ways—a perfectly understandable reaction, because the old lady seemed to spend every hour of every day with her only friend, Walter the mule.

Jamal thought maybe a dog would've been a more sensible choice for a pet. Walter was a stodgy old mule that smelled really, really bad. The smell was a horrible mixture of old, wet wool socks and farts. It was so bad that people could smell Walter even if they were three blocks away!

If you can picture Miss Wilson and Walter together, then you'll know why the other villagers considered them a very odd couple. The old lady always wore big, heavy, dirty work boots and a greasy apron over the same faded print dress. She wore a battered, pinkish, wide-brimmed hat that might have been a fancy-dress Easter hat in its early days. Now it just looked ridiculous. Walter, believe it or not, also wore a hat—a lacy bonnet, like the ones Jamal had seen on babies in old family photos. A bonnet on a mule is a weird enough sight but, somehow, because he was a boy mule wearing a girl's hat, he looked even more unusual.

Jamal had never, not even once, seen Miss Wilson outside without her smelly, funny-looking mule right beside her, nor had he ever seen the old woman with any other human being, because Miss Wilson simply didn't have any friends aside from her mule. Odder still, Miss Wilson talked to Walter almost constantly. Jamal had heard her say things like, "Well, it looks like we're going to get some rain, Walter, what do you think?" and "Oh, what's the matter with these peonies, Walter? Why aren't the petals as soft as the ones from last year?" One time he heard her say, "Get a move on, you old mule!"

But the clincher was that when Miss Wilson spoke to Walter, the mule looked back at her. It seemed to Jamal as though the funny-looking, stinky mule understood every word she said. But, as far as Jamal knew, Walter didn't talk back to her.

Sadly, one summer's day, Miss Wilson's beloved Walter died. Old age probably killed the animal, Jamal figured, because he knew that she had always taken very good care of the mule. Poor Miss Wilson, now she was completely alone. Her only friend in the whole wide world was gone.

Because Jamal delivered the newspaper to Miss Wilson's house every day, he could see that his strange customer was suffering horribly from loneliness after Walter's death. One evening, he talked to his mom and she and several other neighbors got together and decided that what Miss Wilson needed was another mule to keep her company. The very next day, Jamal's mom and some of the other townsfolk approached the woman's cottage.

"We would like to buy you a new mule," they told Miss Wilson when she answered their knocks at her door.

After only a few moments of thought, the lonely old woman told her neighbors, "No. Thank you for your offer, but no other animal could ever replace my Walter."

With that, Miss Wilson quickly and firmly closed her cottage door.

A few months later, in the damp chill of an early spring morning, Jamal was delivering his papers when he came across something that stopped him in his tracks.

What's that? Jamal wondered when he saw what looked like a heap of clothing in Miss Wilson's yard. *Is she getting forgetful? It looks as though she's left her sweater outside overnight. I'd better take it to her door.* He opened the gate to the old woman's backyard, but the sight before him startled Jamal like he'd never been startled before. He just stood there, bewildered. It looked (and smelled!) as if Miss Wilson's old mule, Walter, his bonnet slightly askew, was lying beside her sweater. Jamal knew that what he was seeing and smelling couldn't possibly be real. That animal had died months ago. Worse, closer inspection revealed that it was not just Walter and Miss Wilson's sweater that were in front of him on the ground, but also Miss Wilson herself, who had collapsed in a heap in the sweater.

What should I do? Jamal wondered. *I don't want to go near that spooky mule and I certainly don't want to touch Miss Wilson.* But even if she wasn't dead, she smelled so bad that he didn't want to go any closer to her. *How can they both still smell this horrible when I know that the mule is dead?* Suddenly, Jamal thought of something even more horrible. *What if she's alive now and then she dies while I waste time deciding what to do?*

With a big, deep breath, the boy mustered up all his courage. He set down the bag of newspapers and moved closer to Miss Wilson's almost lifeless body. He crouched down and put his hand on her shoulder. "Miss Wilson! Miss Wilson! What's wrong?" Jamal exclaimed. He was jiggling the woman's arm and hoping desperately that she would come to.

Jamal's fright level skyrocketed when he noticed that Walter's smelly spirit had moved and was now standing right beside him. For a while, the phantom animal looked straight into Jamal's eyes, with his bonnet hanging down over one ear.

Then Walter's ghost slowly trotted off toward the road.

As the mule's apparition reached the curb, it stopped, turned its head back toward Jamal, and looked him straight in the eye once more. For a moment, the newspaper boy and the ghost mule stared at one another. Then the spirit nodded knowingly at Jamal before disappearing completely in about the same amount of time as it takes to blink your eye. Jamal was so upset by what he'd seen, he almost forgot that he still had to help Miss Wilson.

By the time he looked back down at the old woman still lying on the ground, she was opening her eyes. *She's alive!* Jamal thought. After getting Miss Wilson to her feet very slowly, Jamal helped the weakened woman into her house. Then he raced to fetch the town's doctor, who quickly followed the boy back to Miss Wilson's side.

After running some medical tests, the doctor suggested that she had simply not been taking care of herself properly since Walter had died. He was sure that Miss Wilson would recuperate fully within a couple weeks if she rested. And, as it turned out, he was quite correct. Ten days later, Miss Wilson was feeling well enough to work in her garden and to go for walks.

Now, though, Jamal was often at her side. She had told him what had happened, about the fright she had felt when she thought she was going to die in her garden, all alone. She told Jamal how much comfort it had been when she had felt Walter push against her side, and also when she felt his velvety nose as he had nudged it into her palm. She said it had been Walter who had kept her warm until Jamal saved her life.

Miss Wilson lived to be very, very old. And though he always swore that he could smell that terrible stink of Walter around her, Jamal continued to help her. In other words, the ghost of Walter not only rescued Miss Wilson but, in his own ghostly way, he brought her into contact with Jamal, the friend she had needed so badly.

As for Jamal, not only did he enjoy his friendship with the town's strangest living resident, but he was the only one of his friends who could tell a true ghost story when they gathered around the campfire, roasting marshmallows and swapping scary stories.

MONGOOSE MANIFESTATION

The following strange story, which has been reported, documented and investigated over and over again, shows that we don't always have solutions to the mysteries of our world.

The bewildering encounter takes place on the Isle of Man, a small, rugged, windswept piece of land that juts up from the Irish Sea near the northwest coast of England. Such an exceptional setting is just about perfect for this equally exceptional ghost story.

Twelve-year-old Viorrey Irving lived with her parents at an isolated farm on the Isle of Man. Viorrey was a serious girl whose parents were really her only companions.

The Irvings lived in a small stone house, which was not very homey because it was always damp and dark and drafty inside. It wasn't a very comfortable place to live, but at least the family was used to it. Unfortunately, something happened to make the place even less comfortable, especially for young Viorrey.

Early one evening, the girl was in the kitchen washing up for dinner when she heard strange thumping and scurrying sounds. They seemed to come from the ceiling beams directly above her.

"What can be making that noise?" the girl asked her parents.

Immediately, a high, squeaky voice came from the top of the kitchen wall and echoed her exact words.

"What can be making that noise?" the unseen something squealed back at her in an angry, mocking tone.

Viorrey dropped the bar of soap she'd been holding and whirled around to face her parents. The adults must have heard the awful voice too, for their faces showed absolute disbelief and horror. Finally Mr. Irving gathered his senses enough to move. With one sudden lunge to a spot near the back door, he grabbed his rifle, aimed the weapon up toward the ceiling and quickly fired six shots, one right after another. It was only then that Mr.

Irving lowered the gun and waited for whatever he had killed to come crashing down from the rafters to the floor in front of him.

But nothing fell.

The man's voice cracked with fear as he told his wife and daughter, "I saw a pair of beady rodent eyes up there. I aimed directly for them. I must have killed whatever it was."

Viorrey piped up in a shaky voice, "Rodent eyes? You saw a rodent?"

"Yes, I'm sure I did," her father replied.

"A rodent? How could that be? I've never heard of a talking rat before."

The words were no sooner out of the girl's mouth when stones and other strange objects rained down all around them. With Viorrey in the lead, the Irvings fled from the house to safety outside. They stood there, frightened and shaking, for some time. Eventually Viorrey suggested that they all go back inside.

"We can't spend the rest of our lives out here waiting for something to happen," she pointed out to her parents.

To show her parents that they were safe, Viorrey bravely stepped into the darkened interior. She called out "hello," and then jumped back outside when her greeting was returned by a screeching sound coming from near the kitchen ceiling. Then the horrible voice repeated the girl's greeting right back to her. Worse, the echoed words were followed by a bone-chilling cackle filled with evil delight. Whatever was taunting the family clearly hated them.

Viorrey now knew for certain that her home was haunted. And, at that moment, it was not safe for anyone to go into the old stone structure.

The three Irvings sat at the very edge of their property, as far away from the house as they could get. Eventually, Mr. Irving came up with an idea. "I'll make a dose of strong poison," he told his wife and daughter, and he did. After the deadly mixture was ready, the man summoned all his courage and went back into the house. Climbing on a stool and then onto a counter, he spread the poison across the wooden ceiling beams. The potion was strong enough that, if the evil little animal licked its paws after walking over the concoction, he would die immediately. And that, of course, was exactly what the Irvings wanted.

Too bad they didn't know that they could not possibly kill this unnatural enemy because, in fact, the horrid animal's physical body was already dead—and probably had been for many years. As they would eventually learn, the isolated farm family on the Isle of Man was dealing with an unusual ghost—an especially nasty poltergeist.

Poltergeist is a German word that translates into English as "noisy ghost." These rowdy spirits are most often connected with young people—as a matter of fact, young people just about Viorrey's age. It seems as though the energy of preteens and early teens somehow attracts, or possibly even creates, a supernatural force. Poltergeist hauntings are usually strong enough to include sightings and random objects being thrown or moved about. The Irvings' ghost certainly matched this pattern, especially when it was somehow disturbed.

Much to their disappointment, Mr. Irving's powerful poison did not rid the family of their troublemaking intruder. Weeks and then months went by and the Irvings were forced to share their lives with a poltergeist with a very bad attitude. For the most part, the family tried to ignore the mysterious being who had come to stay.

The phantom animal's favorite perch became a rafter in Viorrey's room. The girl began sleeping in the kitchen. By the end of winter, she was eager to return to the privacy of her bedroom. One day, though, when both her parents were out, she decided to try speaking to the presence that was ruining her entire family's life.

Standing in the bedroom doorway, she began to talk to the entity. "We promise not to try to hurt you anymore, if you promise to stop trying to hurt us," she said hesitantly. For several minutes, her words were greeted with nothing but silence. Then, from the darkest corner of the ceiling, Viorrey thought she heard a rustling sound. A moment later, the being's spooky, scratchy voice spoke back.

"I'm not here to hurt you," it began. "If you're nice to me, I'll help you and protect you, but I've been afraid to show myself for fear you'll capture me and never set me free again. I don't want to spend eternity sealed in a bottle, you know. And, by the way, in case you're interested in being courteous, I have a name. I'm Gef."

That night, Viorrey tried as best she could to explain to her parents that she and their house ghost had come to an agreement. She managed to convince both her mother and father to at least try to be nice to their rather sensational visitor from beyond.

"His name is Gef," Viorrey added, hoping that this additional information would make the stranger seem less scary.

Eventually, the adults agreed and for a time, all went well—except when the Irvings had guests. At those times, nothing went well in the cold, haunted stone house on the Isle of Man. When anyone visited, the ghost would screech like a banshee. Nervous neighbors soon spread word through the village that Viorrey and her parents had a ghost.

The Irvings may not have figured out how to get rid of Gef, but Gef had certainly discovered how to get rid of visitors to the house. He simply stole something from each and every person who came into "his" haunt. Not surprisingly, over the weeks, fewer and fewer people dropped in to visit the family. Gef must have liked the peace and quiet because, maybe as a "reward," he began to allow his host family to see him now and then.

After the first sighting, Viorrey's father took an old encyclopedia down from a bookshelf in the stone cottage's main room. He flipped through all the pages from A to M before coming across the information that he wanted. There was even a drawing of the small animal. It looked exactly like Gef! For all the

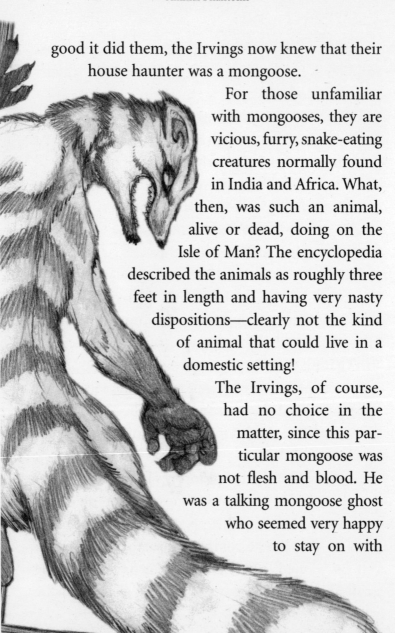

good it did them, the Irvings now knew that their house haunter was a mongoose.

For those unfamiliar with mongooses, they are vicious, furry, snake-eating creatures normally found in India and Africa. What, then, was such an animal, alive or dead, doing on the Isle of Man? The encyclopedia described the animals as roughly three feet in length and having very nasty dispositions—clearly not the kind of animal that could live in a domestic setting!

The Irvings, of course, had no choice in the matter, since this particular mongoose was not flesh and blood. He was a talking mongoose ghost who seemed very happy to stay on with the family forever. The active little spirit obviously liked the cool, humid air and the darkness of the Irvings' home. He must have considered it the best place possible to live out his afterlife.

Every so often, one or other of the Irvings got fed up with Gef and tried to think of a way to get rid of the paranormal nuisance. Attempts to shoot him or poison him certainly hadn't been effective, so one day Viorrey decided to perform a spirit cleansing ceremony in the house—an exorcism. Such a ritual is designed to get ghosts and other supernatural entities to leave a building and pass on through the veil of time into the great beyond. The girl might as well have saved her breath, for her actions only made Gef toss pebbles down from the rafters and ceiling beams that were his supernatural sanctuary.

The Irving family's patience was wearing very thin.

By this time, word of the haunting had spread from the Isle of Man across the sea and into the English cities. Reporters came to investigate the wild tales they'd been hearing. Some even saw the strange ghost and wrote descriptions of Gef in their newspapers. The noisy, bothersome phantom had a "bushy tail like a squirrel's," with "yellow to brownish fur, small ears and a pushed-in face." Some journalists were sure he was a large animal, while others reported a tiny beast. All, however, seemed to agree on the ghostly mongoose's paws, which had three fingers and a thumb.

This last fact was reported to a man named Ivan T. Sanderson, a world-famous naturalist, who declared that such a situation was impossible, that no animal on this earth had such paws.

Other travelers who came to visit the Irvings' haunted house actually heard Gef speak. They made a point of never returning to the stone farmhouse. A few folks who tried to visit were stopped as they entered the front door, when Gef greeted them by heaving pebbles, stones and rocks at them.

Finally, England's renowned National Laboratory of Psychical Research was notified about the strange goings-on. Two experts from the organization made their way to the troubled farmhouse. Gef was decidedly unhappy about this turn of events and responded by screeching to the Irvings, "They'll trap me and put me in a bottle!" From that moment on, the ghost was irritated and extremely active until the two psychics finally and hastily left the area. Only then did the lives of Viorrey and her parents become bearable again—if only for a little while.

Meanwhile, news of the strange haunting had spread to the United States, where someone offered a reward of $50,000 to anyone who could capture Gef and travel with him across America, showing off the otherworldly wonder to all who might be interested. Again, Gef protested, saying that "They'll put me in a bottle!" He hid himself in the darkness of the rafters above Viorrey's bed.

By now, the poltergeist was even more upset than the people he was living with. In order to avoid being captured, the nervous spook kept himself hidden for many years. During this quiet spell, the Irvings sold the farm and moved away from the Isle of Man.

The next owner had been living on the haunted property for less than two years when he reported that he'd clubbed to death a "large black and white, weasel-like animal" that had been stalking his penned chickens. Many people thought that the killing marked the end of Gef, but it's doubtful, because reports of the ghost's size and shape were not at all similar to those of the pest that the new owner killed.

A respected psychic investigator included Gef and the Irvings' story in a book he wrote in the 1950s. There he referred to "the spooks" but wondered if trickery could somehow have been involved. Viorrey, the only member of the Irving family still alive by then, always denied that anyone in the household had created the phantom. As a matter of fact, she said many years later that the ghost's presence had just about ruined their lives during the years that he haunted them.

So great was the effect of the ghostly events that, even to this very day, people on the Isle of Man don't want to talk about the haunting. It seems the whole story still makes them very uneasy.

But what about Gef? When she was last interviewed, Viorrey stated that the mongoose manifestation was seen and heard less and less in the house toward the end of the Irving era. Perhaps it is safe to assume that Gef, the talking mongoose ghost, has finally gone to his eternal reward. Let's hope it wasn't in a bottle!

GHOSTS, ROMANS AND ANCIENT COACHES

Jim Schofield's encounter with ghosts occurred many years ago, but it was such a startling experience that he still remembers it well.

Schofield was driving along a road near a small village in England when he suddenly noticed a big clump of bushes at the roadside moving around as though something was coming through it. Startled, Jim slowed the car a bit and stared at the side of the road. At first he could see absolutely nothing at all. Seconds later, though, he watched in horror as a team of horses suddenly appeared from the underbrush at the side of the road. Slowly, the animals made their way across the road directly in front of his car! Jim stomped on the brake pedal as quickly and as hard as he could, but he knew he was too late. He was already too close to the animals to stop without hitting at least one of the huge horses.

All Jim could do was stare and wait for a horrible accident to unfold. He could see the animals clearly. The look of their saddles left a deep impression on him because he was familiar with horses and riding equipment. But he had never seen anything resembling these saddles. Their shapes, colors and designs were not at all familiar.

Jim's car screeched to a halt but, just as he'd feared, it was not soon enough. His car had hit the last two horses. With his heart pounding in his chest, Schofield jumped out of the car and ran to see what damage had been done—to the horses and to the car. He found nothing. No injured animals, no dead animals. His car's bumper, which should have been crumpled, didn't even have a scratch on it.

The confused man looked around. There were no signs that even one horse, let alone a group of horses, had been anywhere near the area. There were not even any hoof marks in the dirt.

Shaking badly, Schofield got back into his car. He needed to think. What kind of a bizarre encounter had he just witnessed? Slowly Jim Schofield's heart slowed to a normal pace, and that's when he realized

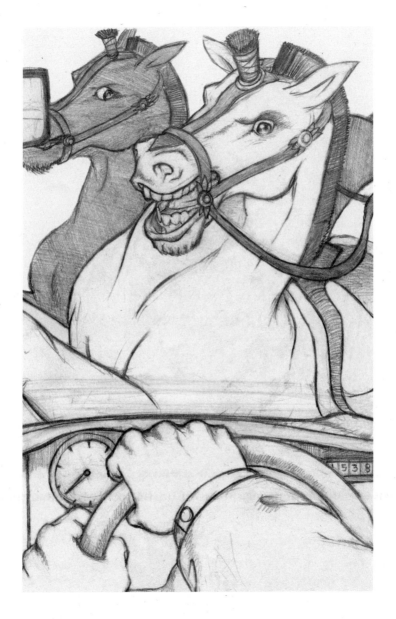

something else that had been puzzling about the sighting. Not only had he never seen saddles like those the horses were wearing, but even the horses themselves looked different. There had to be an explanation. At that moment, though, the man could not think of what the explanation might be.

When he finally felt calm enough to drive again, Jim turned around and headed back home. That evening, he still couldn't erase the bizarre scene from his mind. After considerable thought, the memory of the horses' saddles finally began to make just a little bit of sense to him. He had seen a drawing in a book about ancient times in England when the Romans had invaded. He hurried to his bookshelves, found the book and flipped through the pages until he came to a particular picture. It was a drawing, the likeness of a saddled horse—the kind the Romans had used under Caesar's command in the year 55 BC, when they invaded the British Isles.

Jim knew for certain then that he had experienced a phenomenon known as retrocognition—seeing back into history. *Those were Roman horses I saw, ghosts of steeds ridden through the forests of the English countryside thousands of years ago*, he thought. *They were there and I could see them, but they were not really on this earthly plane with me.*

The only question that remained was whether the Roman horses had come to Jim Schofield or had Jim Schofield somehow found his way back to the exact moment in history when those horses crossed the country road? We'll probably never know. We do know that it was many, many years before the man was ever able to speak of his supernatural encounter.

Perhaps Jim Schofield's mind might have been eased sooner if he had known about the ghostly manifestations at England's Thorpe Hall in Lincolnshire and Borley Rectory, in Essex County, two of the most haunted places in the world. People frequently report hearing horses' hooves and the sounds of wagon wheels crunching along on the gravel path. The sounds come nearer and nearer until they seem to be right in front of the haunted buildings. Then, just as mysteriously and invisibly, the sounds fade off into the distance. Anyone who's heard these bizarre sounds is sure that a horse-drawn coach has just driven past. The trouble is that the same people have seen nothing—nothing at all. These phantom horses and the wagon they pull might be noisy, but they are also invisible.

Something similar happened to three girls walking near Moravian Falls in North Carolina. They swore that they heard the clip-clop of horses' hooves and the rattle of wagon wheels coming up behind them. When they looked where the sounds were coming from, they could see nothing, although the sounds grew louder. Such noises were very familiar to these youngsters because they'd been born and raised in the country. For this reason, the girls moved over farther to the side of the road. They might not be able to see anything yet, but they certainly recognized the sounds well. A horse-drawn wagon was approaching them from behind.

Perhaps a wagon pulled by a horse really was approaching from behind— "behind" in distance but also "behind" in time, for the children listened in fear as they heard (but never saw) the sounds of a phantom horse pulling a phantom wagon.

As soon as the ghosts were gone, the three ran for home. Their parents were very puzzled by their daughters' stories because these girls were normally reliable and dependable. None of them had ever been prone to making up tales. Although the mystery of the invisible horse and wagon was never solved, those girls are adults now and they still staunchly maintain that they were telling the truth.

Anyone who believes in ghosts, of course, would have no trouble solving the mystery!

SCRATCHER

Charlotte and Anita were just as different as two girls could possibly be. Charlotte was tall for her age and very athletic. Anita was always the shortest person in her class and hated all sports, but she was an excellent artist. The girls had lived next door to each other all their lives and had been best friends for as long as either of them could remember. They spent almost all of their spare time together and usually the only friend invited to join them was Scratcher, Charlotte's big orange cat.

One summer a few years ago, Mrs. Larsen, a neighbor across the street, was resting after a stay in the hospital. Although Anita and Charlotte were only 10 years old at the time, they decided to make it their responsibility to help Mrs. Larsen as much as they could. The lady lived alone, except for her cat, and so she really appreciated their company. At least one of the girls visited Mrs. L., as they called her, every afternoon to make sure that she was comfortable and to run errands for her whenever she needed them done. When there were no errands to look after, they just visited the lady for a while and kept her company. Both Charlotte and Anita enjoyed being in Mrs. Larsen's tiny, crowded house and they really liked to play with Mooch, her big, gray and white cat.

Each day over the summer, Mrs. Larsen seemed to be getting a bit stronger, until the morning that Anita arrived at Mrs. Larsen's house and found the woman in tears. It seemed that Mooch, her only full-time companion, had died during the night. What made the sad situation even worse was that the cat had apparently been killed on purpose, poisoned by some heartless fool. Anita did everything she could to comfort the grieving woman, but nothing seemed to help. As Anita told Charlotte later in the day, it was as though Mrs. Larsen's heart had broken.

"This is horrible!" Charlotte replied, unable to understand why anyone would kill an innocent cat, especially one owned by someone who had never done a mean thing in her life. "So sad and senseless."

The girls and their parents buried the cat's body under a tree in Mrs. Larsen's backyard and tried to comfort the woman. When the bad news spread up and down the tree-lined street, all of the neighbors tried to help the broken-hearted woman feel better. Despite their efforts, Mrs. Larsen was never really happy, or well, again. She died just a few weeks later.

Neither Anita nor Charlotte enjoyed summer much after that. They kept to themselves even more than usual and were mostly just waiting for school to start so they'd have more activities to keep them from being sad about Mrs. Larsen's death.

"At least Mrs. Larsen and Mooch are together again," Charlotte's mother often told the girls in an attempt to help to cheer them up.

More than anything or anyone else, Scratcher, Charlotte's cat, helped the girls get over some of their sorrow. The adorable cat was always eager to play and that usually managed to distract them. Scratcher was an especially clever cat and as full of personality as could be. He was lots of fun to be with because he loved being fussed over. As a matter of fact, "The Scratch" had only one bad habit. He loved to roam. Often the adventuresome kitty did not come back from his journeys for days and days. At first, Charlotte would worry about this but, because the wanderer always came home eventually, she soon became used to her pet being away.

When summer ended that year, both Charlotte and Anita were anxious for the new school year to begin. Little did the girls know, but they had big changes ahead. For the first time since kindergarten, they were in different classrooms. Although they vowed that they'd always be best friends, by the time Christmas break came around, they each had lots of new interests and lots of new friends. Their friendship with one another had become less and less important. By the time the school year ended, the two girls hardly ever saw one another.

One evening as Charlotte was getting ready for bed, she realized that she hadn't seen Scratcher all day. The thought didn't bother her much, though, because she was sure the roaming cat would soon be home safe and sound as he always was.

Next door, Anita was already in her pajamas. She had been sitting in her bedroom reading when she suddenly noticed something moving in her room. She didn't know what it could have been, but she did know that the movement came from over in the corner. She swung her head around to see what had managed to get into her room, even though the door and window were firmly closed. One glance assured her that everything was fine and nothing was moving. *Must have been my imagination, I guess,* Anita thought and turned her attention back to her book—for a second.

Out of the corner of her eye, the girl saw another sudden motion. This one didn't vanish. At first, it just looked like a slight stirring in the air above her desk. Then, the odd waviness transformed itself into speckles. As the girl watched, the extraordinary speckles multiplied and began to form an image.

Too frightened to move or even to call out, Anita watched as a strange, supernatural scene developed before her eyes. Seconds later, as clear as though she was standing on the sidewalk and not sitting in her bed, Anita saw a tree-lined road. She recognized the place immediately. It was a street just south of her neighborhood.

As she stared at the vision before her eyes, she could see a white Volkswagen Bug approaching. The car careened around the street corner so fast that it nearly tipped over. Just then an orange cat appeared on the sidewalk. It was Scratcher! The moment the speeding car came near the spot where Scratcher was standing, the cat dashed out onto the street. The Bug's driver slammed on his brakes and stopped. But it was too late. His car had run over Charlotte's much-adored cat. The results were fatal.

Leaving his Bug still idling, the driver walked back and looked at the cat's broken body on the road. He lifted Scratcher's corpse and put it at the side of the road before driving away—again at top speed. Tears were running down Anita's cheeks as she continued to watch the horrible events unfold before her eyes.

Soon, a man driving an old pick-up truck came along. He spotted the cat's dead body, stopped his truck and got out. First, he checked to see if there was any hope of saving the animal. When the man realized that the cat was dead, he picked up the corpse that had once been Scratcher and placed it gently on the seat of his truck. In horrid fascination, Anita continued to watch the scenes taking place before her eyes. With the dead cat beside him, the man slowly drove away from the scene of the terrible accident.

Desperate to free herself from this gruesome and tragic scene she was being forced to watch, Anita tried to scream for her parents, but no sound came from her throat. The paranormal vision continued. She watched as the truck driver slowly steered toward a park near the schoolyard. Once there, the man got out of his truck, took a shovel from behind the front seat and proceeded to dig a small shallow grave in a corner of the park near a tree. When the hole was deep enough, he placed the cat's body in it and shoveled the loose earth back into place.

Then, as quickly as the ghostly images had appeared to Anita, they were gone.

Finally, the frightened girl's voice came back to her. "What was that?" she said out loud to the empty room. "What have I just seen? Should I tell Charlotte? No, I can't. What if what I saw was real? But, it couldn't have been. It must've been my imagination playing tricks. I can't mention this to anyone—not to Charlotte and certainly not to my parents. Not yet, anyway."

The next morning on the way to school, Anita made a point to catch up to Charlotte so they could walk together. Anita had already decided that if her friend mentioned anything about Scratcher being missing then she would try to explain the strange vision she'd had the night before. If Charlotte didn't say anything, she wouldn't either. The girls chatted on the way to school—it was just about like old times—but cats were not mentioned.

That night, much to her dismay, Anita had another ghostly visitation. This time the waves in the air above her desk became flecks of light. Slowly, they came together to form a human image—the image of Mrs. Larsen—or at least the ghost of her. The woman's spirit was tenderly holding two cats, Mooch and Scratcher. The scene before Anita's eyes was so comforting that it soothed away all the fear she had been feeling. The girl knew that she'd just had a very special experience, a chance that very few people, children or adults, ever get—a peek through the curtain of time that usually separates the living from the dead.

The next day, Anita realized that she had no alternative but to tell Charlotte about the supernatural sights she'd somehow been allowed to view. Once again, she caught up to her old friend on the way to school. Without waiting for as much as a "hi" or "good morning" from her friend, Anita blurted out all of the details she could remember about the visions she'd witnessed.

Charlotte stood still, upset and confused by the bizarre news. She knew her old friend would not lie to her, but how could any of this possibly be true? The girls decided that there was only one way to be sure that Anita's ghostly visions had been real. They turned away from the direction of the school and walked toward the street where Anita was sure Scratcher had been killed. About halfway along that block, they stopped. Both girls cried out as they looked at the road. There were blood-stains on the pavement—right at the spot where Anita had somehow seen the white Volkswagen run over the orange cat.

Slowly and quietly, the two turned away. They walked to the park near the schoolyard, knowing exactly what they would find. Sadly, they were correct, for near a tree they saw a small mound of loose earth. It was the final resting place of the adventuresome Scratcher's earthly remains. Without saying a word, the girls left the mound untouched, turned and made their way to school.

When the principal saw how upset the two were, she immediately offered to drive them home. Anita chose to stay at school in the hopes that all the goings-on there would distract her from all the terrible experiences she'd had over the past few days. Charlotte, however, gratefully accepted the woman's offer and spent the rest of her day quietly at home.

Over the next few weeks, Charlotte tried to get used to life without Scratcher. It was difficult, because she missed her cat terribly. One morning as the girl was heading out to school, she stopped and called on her friend Anita.

"Want to walk with me?" she asked.

Anita nodded and the two went off together.

"You know," Charlotte began. "I really want to get another cat to keep me company, but I'm scared that somehow, even though he's dead, it would hurt Scratcher's feelings. I don't know what to do."

"Maybe wait a little while longer," Anita suggested in a quiet voice. "You can't be over The Scratch's death yet. I know that I still have nightmares about the ghosts I saw when he died and I still miss him a lot, too, even though he was your cat, not mine."

Charlotte looked at her friend for a moment and then asked, "Do you think we'll ever know what caused those phantom visions?"

"Probably not," Anita replied, "but I do know that they were real."

Another week passed and still Charlotte couldn't bring herself to tell her parents that she wanted to get another pet. Anita was still trying to push her glimpse of the world beyond into the back of her mind, when Mrs. Larsen's spirit appeared to her one final time. The spectral woman looked radiant as she lovingly held both cats, but this time she spoke.

"Scratcher is a little sweetheart," the ghost said. "He is bringing one of his kittens to Charlotte."

The next day, a neighbor knocked on Charlotte's door. "My cat has just given birth to a litter of kittens and by the looks of them I'm sure your cat is the father. The only male in the litter looks exactly like him. I heard that your cat had been killed. I'd like to give you his son if you'd like another cat."

Charlotte was overjoyed. Six weeks later, when the kittens were ready to leave their mother, she went over to her neighbor's home to pick up her furry new friend. When she saw the tiny cat that was to be hers, she could hardly believe her eyes. He was an exact miniature of Scratcher!

She named her new kitten, Sonny.

As Sonny grew, Charlotte noticed that it had many of his father's personality quirks. There was one quality, though, that the little cat did not share with Scratcher. The older cat had always been anxious to roam, but the kitten never once showed any interest in venturing out beyond his own fenced yard. Charlotte and Anita always wondered if that was because Scratcher's ghost was watching over his son. Or maybe, in his first life, The Scratch had learned his lesson about the dangers of roaming.

Perhaps this new cat was not actually Scratcher's son at all, but rather Scratcher himself returning to enjoy a second, longer life—in complete safety.

FOREVER HAUNTED

For those of us who live in North America, India seems a world away—an almost magical place. The country bustles with crowds of exotically dressed people, brilliant colors, lush vegetation, unfamiliar sounds and smells. Tourists in India have so much to see and hear and taste and smell and touch that it can become too much to deal with and people have been known to get horribly confused and frightened.

During World War II, American soldiers were often stationed for a few days at a military camp near the city of Calcutta. Because this place was so different than any place most of them had ever been before, the soldiers were often extremely uneasy in their temporary home. Richard was one such soldier. Many years after the war was over and he was safely back home in the United States, Richard remembered exactly how terror-stricken he had been during his first-ever guard duty there.

Even the trek to get to the temporary military quarters had not made any of the soldiers in Richard's unit feel at home. They had made their way through thick vines and other natural growth. On their way, they passed by spooky-looking, tumbled-down remains of ancient buildings, including a pile of rocks and stones that had once been a temple. The eerie hike, through dark and damp territory, had been accompanied by strange and unfriendly noises.

Once the soldiers arrived at the camp, two were chosen to keep watch for the night while the others slept. Richard was one of those ordered to stand guard. As he was part of a unit that paired soldiers with trained dogs, the young man would at least have his dog to keep him company during the overnight watch. On the other side of the camp, another soldier and his dog would be doing the same.

As he paced around the part of the camp he had been ordered to patrol, Richard was disgusted to discover flying insects, crawling bugs, quirky lizards and slithering snakes. *How much worse can this night get?* he might have wondered. If so, he was about to find out in a particularly eerie supernatural way, because the noises and movements that had been making him feel so very uncomfortable stopped all at once. They simply stopped. Complete silence and stillness encircled him. Seconds later, the dog by his side and the others dogs in their pen began to shift about restlessly. The animals squirmed and whimpered as though they were newborn pups instead of the intelligent, specially chosen and highly trained adult dogs that they were.

Richard reached down to give his own dog a reassuring pat, but yanked his arm back up again quickly when he could feel the hair on the back of the animal's neck standing straight up. He could hear a vicious growl build in its throat. Still having no idea what was happening or what he should do to save himself or his fellow soldiers, Richard slowly turned around. He thought he'd heard a sound—from far off in the distance. He listened as the noise grew louder and louder until he finally recognized it. It was the thundering of horses' hooves galloping toward the camp at top speed. A herd of steeds was charging toward him from the direction of the old crumbled temple they had passed on their route into the base.

With his heart in his throat, Richard drew his gun. But what could he shoot at? Nothing was visible in the inky black that surrounded the terrified soldier, but still the terrible sounds pounded louder and louder against his eardrums. Dozens of stampeding horses were charging directly at him. The hooves of the galloping herd made the ground beneath his feet vibrate. With that new sensation, Richard gave up trying to be strong. There was no way, on his own, that he was going to be able to do his job and protect the others. Peoples' lives were in dreadful danger. He would have no alternative but to sound the alarm.

And he no doubt would have done so if he'd had time, because Richard had no sooner reached that decision than his dog reared up and lunged against its leash with such force that it sent Richard flying face first, flat on the ground. As the man lay there, paralyzed with fear, he felt a great rush of cool, damp wind whirl past him. That midnight in the Indian jungle near Calcutta, Richard listened, terror stricken, as dozens of horses headed directly toward him as he lay in the dirt.

Mere seconds before the young man was sure he was going to faint from fear, the sounds began to recede into the distance on the other side of the camp until the thundering hooves were mere whisperings once again. Then, just as suddenly as the noises had begun, they stopped—all at once and absolutely completely. He had not seen a thing—not even one horse—nor had he been hurt, let alone killed.

The immediate danger had apparently passed, but Richard's fright hadn't. It took him days afterward to calm down. His friends asked over and over what it was that was bothering him, but the man would not say a word about his terrible supernatural encounter with the spirit horses. Such an admission would invite dreadful teasing at the very least.

Less than a week after the soldier's experience with the paranormal, Richard heard some interesting local history. It seems that the tumbled-down temple near the base camp was thought to be an evil place. Those who lived in the area would not go near the ruins. They had seen and heard hundreds of the different ghosts that haunted it—including charging horses. Memories of these haunting experiences never left them.

Richard knew then that, on a dark night during his World War II guard duty in India, he had become, and would remain, one of those haunted people.

AN EXTRAORDINARY TALE

When is a ghost cat not the ghost of a cat? Perhaps the answer to that riddle might be hidden in this very strange but true story—which begins like a fairy tale.

A long time ago in St. Louis, Missouri, Marcus and Jessica Meriwether lived like a king and queen. Their house was a mansion so big that it was almost a palace.

Aside from the servants who worked for them, the Meriwethers lived alone. They never had any children. As a matter of fact, they had never even had so much as a pet goldfish to keep them company. They did have many friends, though, and they were very content with their lives.

Sadly, Jessica died one summer day. Everyone who knew the Meriwethers wondered, at first, if Marcus would be able to manage without his beloved wife. People feared that, even with all his wealth, the man might become a hermit—living alone and never leaving his enormous house. They needn't have worried, because it wasn't long before Mr. Meriwether was back to many of his old routines.

A few months after his wife's funeral, Marcus Meriwether was asked to give a speech to an important group of people. No one knew for certain if he'd be able to do it. After all, he might still be too sad for anything like public speaking. As the date of the speech drew closer, the organizers decided to check and see if Mr. Meriwether was still willing to talk to the group.

"If you don't feel well enough to make the speech, please just tell us. We can make other arrangements and will certainly understand if you think it would be too much for you," they advised.

"I'll be all right," Meriwether replied. "Besides, I know this is something Jessica would have wanted me to do."

The day of the big speech dawned bitterly cold. By evening a raging snowstorm had moved into the city. The weather was so bad that everyone, it seemed, was staying home that night. Despite the terrible conditions, Mr. Meriwether was determined to get to the meeting. He had his chauffeur bring the car around to the front of the house. He sat in the back of his limousine as his trusted employee drove cautiously through the blizzard to the downtown hotel where the surprisingly large audience had gathered to hear him speak.

As his chauffeur came around to open the car door for the man, Mr. Meriwether did up his coat, put on his gloves, pulled down his hat and wound his scarf once more around his neck before stepping out onto the sidewalk in front of the building. Just as his feet touched on the snowy sidewalk beneath him, a cat, of all things, appeared beside him. The animal stood still for a second and then in one swift motion leaped on to Marcus Meriwether's shoulder.

The man called out in shock. His chauffeur and the hotel's doorman came running to see what the problem was. They grabbed the cat off the startled man's shoulder and tossed the animal into a snow bank.

"I'm so sorry, sir," the doorman said. "I can't imagine where that cat came from. I hope you're not hurt."

"No, no, I'm not hurt at all. That was rather strange, wasn't it?" Meriwether replied.

"Indeed," the other man agreed. "I have worked here for years and I have never seen that cat before. Frankly, I don't think I've ever seen any cat anywhere that big. I can't imagine where it might have come from. I do apologize for not having seen the animal in time to prevent it from jumping up on you."

As he made his way across to the hotel lobby, Meriwether muttered, "No harm done."

In spite of the terrible snowstorm and the strange encounter with the cat, Marcus Meriwether gave an excellent speech and, by the time the evening ended, everyone was pleased. The doorman saw the speaker preparing to leave the building and signaled the man's chauffeur to bring the limousine to the curb. But, just as the driver opened the car door for his master, that same enormous cat suddenly reappeared and once more pounced up onto Meriwether's shoulder. They both tried to pull its claws loose from the cloth of Meriwether's overcoat, but the cat held on tightly.

"Oh, my goodness, sir," the doorman spluttered. "I am so sorry. Nothing like this has ever happened before! I don't know what to say."

Much to everyone's surprise, Meriwether commanded, "Leave the animal alone. It's a dreadful night. The cat may die if we leave her out. I'll take her home with me for now. My maid can care for her overnight and then deal with her properly in the morning."

And so, with the cat still perched on his shoulder, Marcus Meriwether somewhat awkwardly settled himself into the back of his car. As soon as the chauffeur pulled onto the street, the cat carefully moved to the seat beside Mr. Meriwether and there she sat, still and completely quiet, for the entire drive home.

Mr. Meriwether also sat motionless and silent. He paid no attention to the cat. Not once did he stroke the animal or speak to her. He did note that the doorman's assessment had been correct. This peculiar feline was huge, the largest cat Meriwether had ever seen. It wasn't until they were at home under the glow of the electric lights that the man also realized she was an exquisitely beautiful cat. Her coat was a rich golden color and her tail was nothing short of extraordinary—thick and soft in an even deeper, gold color.

"Care for this pathetic creature," Meriwether instructed the chauffeur. The chauffeur carried the cat into the back of the house and immediately gave her to the maid, repeating the instructions. Marcus took his coat and boots off and made himself comfortable in an easy chair by the fireplace.

Moments after he sat down, the cat walked into the room with her head and tail held high. She hopped effortlessly up onto the arm of Meriwether's chair and she sat there, as still as could be, for the rest of the evening. Just as he had done in the car, the man completely ignored the animal. He did not pet her. He did not speak to her. He did not even look at her.

Knowing that their employer did not like animals, the servants tried to keep the cat away from Mr. Meriwether. They could not. Wherever Meriwether went, the cat soon followed. The only time the animal went with any member of the staff was when they answered the door to visitors. It was almost, the maids thought, as though this strange cat wanted to greet the guests as they arrived. Every one of those guests commented upon the enormous and beautiful cat. They were even more intrigued when they saw the animal sitting with such great dignity on the arm of Meriwether's chair as the man chatted with them.

Although no one would make such a comment while they were in the mansion, many visitors admitted after that they found the animal's eyes to be very eerie. They were piercing, intent cat's eyes. Impossible as it might have been, those eyes looked human. They made the big, beautiful cat look as though she understood all that was going on around her.

Sometimes, just for the fun of it, the maids who were responsible for feeding the cat occasionally tried to get her to play. They never even once succeeded. The feline would just put her chin up, turn her beautiful tail toward them and walk away.

For years, life at the Meriwether mansion went on exactly this way. The cat didn't change her behavior, nor did Mr. Meriwether—at least not until September 1952, when Marcus Meriwether remarried.

From that day forward, no one ever saw the remarkable stray cat again. She simply disappeared the day the man took another wife. Her disappearance was just as sudden as her appearance had been that winter night shortly after Meriwether's first wife's death.

Some might think this quite a mystery, but others might ask, "When is a ghost cat not the ghost of a cat"? The answer to that conundrum might be, when that ghost cat is actually the ghost of Mrs. Jessica Meriwether.

Now isn't that an extraordinary thought?

THE GIANT DEER

Sixteen-year-old Anthony was smiling as he set out on his first-ever week of hunting all on his own. It had taken him months to talk his mother into letting him take this trip to California's Kelso Valley. Anthony suspected that it was only because he'd been so disappointed about not getting into the military academy that his mother had changed her mind and let him go. She knew that he'd worked hard at cadet school, but apparently there were 20 other kids who were better than he was because they would be attending the academy and Anthony wouldn't.

Getting into that school had been Anthony's goal for two years. When he didn't win a spot on the academy's student list, he just felt like giving up on everything. After what seemed like forever, Anthony noticed that he was feeling just a bit happier with each passing day. He started thinking about how good it would be to get away all on his own for a while. Then he could prove to himself that he wasn't a failure even though he'd only be attending his local high school.

The day that his mother finally agreed to let him go on his adventure was the first day Anthony felt really good since the academy turned him down. Once again, he had something to work toward. There was lots of planning and preparation for any hunting trip and the first one alone was especially important. The night before he left for his week away, Anthony could hardly sleep. Even though he was excited and a bit anxious, he knew he could handle everything involved with the trip. After all, he'd been on dozens of hunting trips with groups from the hunting club he belonged to. He just wanted get started.

By daybreak the next morning he was on his way and two hours later he arrived at Watsonville, the town nearest the valley. Anthony knew from all the expeditions he'd taken with the hunting club that he could get his last-minute food and supplies right there. It would be his only stop before making his way into the wilderness where he'd have nothing to rely on but his brains and courage and skill.

As he entered the darkened store, the man behind the counter greeted him with a friendly wave. Anthony knew exactly where to find everything he needed because he'd always watched the club's leaders carefully when they had come in for supplies. Shortly, Anthony headed to the cash register, juggling his purchases.

"You new around here?" the man behind the counter asked as he bagged Anthony's canned heat, biscuits, bottled water and dried fruit.

"Just visiting, sir," Anthony answered politely. "I'm going hunting for deer down in the valley."

The man nodded but didn't say anything.

"Aren't you going to warn him about the ghost?" a voice from behind the stacks of camping gear called out.

Anthony was the only customer in the store so he knew the comment had been made to him. "Ghost?" he asked trying not to laugh.

The clerk by the cash register handed Anthony's purchases to him and said, "I wasn't going to mention the ghost. You don't seem like a guy who would take such a legend seriously, anyway."

"You're right, I'm not. Well, I certainly don't believe in any kind of ghosts. But, now that you've mentioned it, I am curious. What is this legend you're talking about?" Anthony asked, grinning, still half thinking the men in the store were teasing him because he was so young. He'd show them. He may not have been able to get into military school, but he was still a pretty tough fellow.

"You'd better tell him," the voice from the aisle urged.

Anthony nodded enthusiastically and, with a bit of a chuckle, the man by the cash register began to tell the tale. "There's an old ghost story around here, my friend. It's about a phantom deer that's said to haunt the valley. I've never seen the animal myself, but I've talked to people who have. They say the beast is the size of two deer. They also say he can't be killed. Legend or not, if I were you, I'd watch out for that animal when I'm in the valley."

Anthony was quiet for a moment. He'd never believed in ghosts at all and certainly not in the ghosts of giant animals! He told the man just exactly that.

"I don't believe in the supernatural or spirits or whatever it is you're talking about. I do believe, though, that I'm a pretty good shot," the teenager assured the storekeeper. "I think that if I had a target as big as that deer, I'd have a trophy hanging on my wall in no time."

"Suit yourself," the man replied and said no more.

Anthony picked up his purchases and headed out the door. "Good-bye," he said.

"Good luck," came the reply.

Well, that was a strange shopping trip, he thought as he left. With a snort of laughter, Anthony drove his truck down into the valley and chose a campsite. He immediately got busy setting up his tent, storing his food and making his campsite comfortable. By then, Anthony had all but forgotten the strange tale the men in the grocery store had told him.

Once his campsite was prepared, Anthony sat down to enjoy being outdoors without an adult anywhere nearby. Just at that moment, though, he caught a glimpse of something moving among the trees. He grabbed his rifle and peered through its telescope. At first, he couldn't see anything in the dense thicket. Then he scanned the area more slowly and carefully. And that's when Anthony saw it—a deer so big that he wanted it more than anything he'd ever wanted in his entire life. He knew that it couldn't be the deer from that ridiculous ghost story the men in the grocery store had told him about. For one thing, no such phantom could exist, and people who believed in foolishness like spirits and ghosts and phantoms and the like always said that you could see right through the ghostly bodies.

"Wow," Anthony said aloud before he realized that he had actually spoken. *Mustn't make any noise. I don't want anything to scare this beauty away. Everyone will be envious when I bag this giant. I know I can do it,* he thought as he tried to control his jitters. He'd need calm, quiet breathing and steady hands to hit his target. He stood still, took aim, pulled the trigger and, holding his breath, stared as the bullet flew directly into the enormous animal's heart.

Anthony had done enough hunting that he knew for certain that he'd scored a direct hit. He also knew that the huge animal had to be dead. No deer, no matter how large,

could survive a bullet as fast, accurate and powerful as the one he had just fired.

Anthony was delighted with himself. He got the animal with his first shot. A clean kill. He would worry about how to get the giant deer's corpse out of the brush and back to his campsite after he'd inspected his bounty.

As he approached the underbrush where his prey had stood, Anthony looked for the giant's tracks. There were none—no hoof prints in the dry ground, no branches broken from when the animal had trudged through. Even where Anthony's trophy should have fallen, there was nothing. Not even the smallest twig was broken or bent. Stranger still was that the young man could not see even a trace of blood from the fatal wound. Strangest of all, however, was that the body of the animal was nowhere to be seen. It was as if the giant deer had never existed.

Too freaky, Anthony thought with a shiver. *I shot that animal right in the heart. Where is it? This is impossible!* He turned around. *I must have killed it, but where is it? And why is it so quiet here all of a sudden? I can't hear anything. Nothing. This is eerie. I'm getting out of here!*

But then Anthony remembered how much he would enjoy bragging about killing the deer. Nervously he searched again, but by then he was just too badly spooked. *Something very creepy's going on here. It was real. I shot it. I killed it, I know I did. But now I can't find any trace of it. The silence around here is creeping me out.*

Unfortunately, when he arrived back at his camp-site and realized that the wind had picked up and life in the brush had returned to normal, Anthony still couldn't stop thinking what had happened. In fact, he began to get more and more afraid. He jumped every time he heard a sound. He flinched every time a branch moved. Confused, disappointed and afraid, Anthony packed up his camping gear and drove back toward town.

He stopped at a diner on the main road. As Anthony sat in the restaurant, he began to feel better. *I must have been imagining that enormous deer,* he told himself. *I've already failed at one thing this year. I'm not going to let this one beat me. I'm going to go back. I've planned this trip for ages. I'll be sorry for the rest of my life if I let a bit of kidding put me off my goal.*

A few seconds later, though, the teenager remembered the unnatural, haunting stillness in the forest while he searched for his downed deer. Anthony shook his head and tried to focus on other things. Fortunately, a few seconds later the waitress came by to take his order.

"Hamburger and fries, please," the young hunter told the woman. He paused for just a moment and then said, "I want to ask you a question, Miss. Have you ever heard anyone from around here talk about a giant deer?"

"You mean down in the valley? Yah, sure. That's the ghost deer. He's been around for more years than anyone can count. My granddad used to tell us about it. Is the animal still there? I haven't heard anyone mention him yet this year. I didn't know if a ghost could survive that last winter. It was bad enough to kill the dead."

Anthony must have looked surprised because the waitress added, "Well, of course, no one knows for certain if that giant deer was ever really alive. There's no one left around these parts who's old enough to remember. All of us, even back to Granddad, have just known him as a ghost. He is a huge animal, though, isn't he?"

Anthony could not even reply. The waitress saw the expression on his face. She was used to such expressions from people just learning about the deer's ghost because she'd lived in this area all her life and knew about people's reactions after catching a glimpse of the legendary phantom.

"I'll get you your food now," she added before turning and walking away from Anthony.

When his food came, he ate in silence. He'd made up his mind. He was disappointed about it, but he was definitely going to go home. He would never tell anyone about his encounter with the ghost.

As he set off for home, Anthony thought that perhaps his hunting trip hadn't been a failure after all. *I've seen something that none of my friends have, even if they've been accepted into the academy. I've seen something that tells me the supernatural world really does exist.* Anthony became uncomfortable with the thought that he'd tried to kill that legendary animal. He realized that he never wanted to go hunting again. He would give his rifle back to the club and take up another hobby. Anthony decided that his new hobby would be rebuilding old cars. It's a good thing Anthony didn't know that old cars are often haunted.

WITCH OR WEREWOLF?

All the townsfolk in the small English village of Ashton knew about their strange and mysterious neighbor, Mrs. Prouse. Frankly, she made her neighbors nervous. She was a big, heavy-set woman with long, messy hair, and she had the strangest eyes anyone had ever seen—one eye was green and the other was yellow.

The villagers wondered, too, about her odd collections of things, for no one else in town had a supply of bat wings, snake eyes, dried toads or bird feathers on hand, to say nothing of the array of odd-looking containers she kept them in. One particularly curious container was a three-handled cup—the likes of which no one in those parts had ever seen before.

Many people readily admitted that Mrs. Prouse scared them. Others maintained that, although the old lady did make them nervous, Mrs. Prouse was nothing but a crazy fool and was not to be feared. But all agreed that if they were troubled—about their health, their romances, their crops or anything else that might not be right—Mrs. Prouse was the person to see. Often, after just one meeting with the old woman, their problems were gone.

Depending on the complaint, Mrs. Prouse might sing a chant as she boiled dried animal bones in a cauldron or she might hang up scary-looking dolls with pins sticking into them. Still other times, the weird old lady might have her guest drink a dreadful-tasting tea that she had prepared from some awful-smelling powder and served in her curious three-handled cup. Whatever remedy she gave them, Mrs. Prouse's patients soon found their problems had flown away like a witch on a broomstick.

Women often sought her advice because, in spite of her age, Mrs. Prouse's skin was beautifully, almost unnaturally, smooth—as silky as a baby's. Of course, this quirk only added to the villagers' nervousness about what powers she might actually have. One day, though, the curious folks suddenly forgot their fascination with the strange old lady. That was the day after the first sighting of the phantom wolf.

It wasn't just the strange animal's howling that disturbed the people of Ashton, for they were used to sleeping through the sounds of wolves baying at the moon. No, this noise was more troubling, louder and definitely more mournful.

After only a few nights of the eerie racket, villagers armed with rifles headed out to hunt down the troublesome beast. One of their shots struck a penetrating blow into the animal's leg and the beast limped away, whimpering horribly.

Mrs. Prouse was seen in town the next day. Oddly, she was limping badly. Everyone noticed this eerie coincidence, and by noon the entire village population was abuzz with gossip. The bravest man in town was chosen to ask the old woman why she was favoring her left leg.

"I cut myself while I was chopping wood," she replied curtly, before using her good leg to drag herself off.

When the eerie baying sounds had not been heard for a number of nights, a small group of curious folk decided to pay a visit to the dilapidated Prouse cottage. The gate to the creepy old place was rusty and screeched, nay, almost howled, in loud protest when it was opened. Weeds had grown around the house until they were so high that they almost blocked the front door.

Two people held back the tangled overgrowth while a third person pushed open the entranceway and stepped inside. The house was empty. Empty of anything alive, that is. The smell of something decaying lingered, and it was so strong that it seemed to have a life of its own. No combination of rude words could describe the terrible stench that wafted out of the dark and gloomy place.

Filled with equal parts of determination, courage, fear and fascination, the frightened trio went into the rundown old house. Just seconds later, their bravery gone, all three ran to escape from the horrid house. Still, no one could say exactly where the smell came from.

The very next day, the trio returned. This time they were accompanied by dozens of other villagers—anyone willing to take the terrifying risk of visiting the unnatural place. The group silently approached the gate, each person dreading what he or she was about to see.

Mrs. Prouse's house was simply not there. It had disintegrated, its timbers rotted and fallen.

"This land is cursed!" one man cried out.

"It is evil!" shouted another.

"It is haunted!" screamed a third before the villagers fled from the spooky scene.

Years later a newcomer moved onto the abandoned land where the strange old cottage had once stood. While cleaning decades of debris out of the overgrown well-shaft, the man came across a skeleton—a very strange skeleton. Some of the bones appeared to be from a dog or a wolf. Others were human. A bullet lay imbedded in one leg bone and, lying beside the bizarre arrangement of bones, was a strange-looking cup—a cup with three handles. The man did not touch either the cup or any of the bones. The sight filled him with such dread that he fled immediately and settled somewhere else.

To this day, the land on which Mrs. Prouse lived lies abandoned—by the living, that is. Perhaps it shouldn't be too surprising. After all, wolves and witches have long been associated with each other. They are called werewolves.

Was Mrs. Prouse a witch? Was she a phantom wolf? Was she a werewolf? Was she a ghost of a wolf, come back in the human form of a spooky old woman? And even though everyone else who drank out of the three-handled cup found their troubles went away, how come Mrs. Prouse's troubles didn't— but *she* did?

Today we are unlikely to solve this paranormal puzzle, but if you ever see a three-handled cup, don't touch it!

SOURCES

The following sources provided direct or indirect inspiration for the stories in this volume.

Alexander, John. *Ghosts: Washington's Most Famous Ghost Stories.* Arlington, Virginia: The Washington Book Trading Company, 1988.

Bardens, Dennis. *Ghosts and Hauntings.* New York: Ace Book, 1965.

Fate Magazine, January 1969; September 1956; April 1972.

Holzer, Hans. *Psychic Investigator.* New York: Popular Library, 1970.

Hurl, Karen, and Janet Bord. *Ghosts.* Glasgow, Scotland: Harper Collins, 2000.

Macklin, John. *Dimensions Beyond the Unknown.* New York: Ace Books, 1968.

Macklin, John. *A Look Through Secret Doors.* New York: Ace Publishing, 1969.

Mysteries of the Unknown: Hauntings. Alexandria, Virginia: Time-Life Books, 1989.

Smith, Warren. *Into the Strange.* New York: Popular Library, 1968.

Tralins, Robert. *Supernatural Strangers.* New York: Popular Library, 1970.

USA Weekend Editors. *I Never Believed in Ghosts Until.* Chicago: Contemporary Books, 1992.

Webb, Robert. *Voices from Another World: True Tales of Occult.* New York: Manor Books, 1972.

ACKNOWLEDGMENTS

It is a privilege to thank *everyone* associated with Ghost House Books. Your support has meant so much to me over the years. Special thanks to Grant Kennedy, Shane Kennedy, Nancy Foulds, Shelagh Kubish, Curtis Pillipow, Gerry Dotto, Elliot Engley, Chris Wangler, Aaron Norell and everyone else involved in the creation of this book. Please know that I am well aware that if you didn't do what you do, I couldn't do what I do! Thank you.

I would also like to express my gratitude to Bonnie Robbins of Brandon, Manitoba, and W. Ritchie Benedict of Calgary—both researchers extraordinaire. Your generosity warms my heart.

And, finally, heartfelt thanks to the people who make up the core of my world: Bob, Debbie, Robyn, Jo-Anne and Barrie. Together you form my safety net. Thank you for being your loving and supportive selves.

Ghost House Books

COLLECT THE WHOLE SERIES!

Add to your Ghost House collection with these books full of
fascinating mysteries and terrifying tales.

Ghost Riders: True Ghost Stories of Planes, Trains and Automobiles
by Barbara Smith

You can take this spine-chilling collection of scary stories with you on your
next road trip. Barbara Smith shares eyewitness accounts of encounters
with the unexplained aboard different modes of transportation, including
a mysterious model airplane that provides an eerie warning and a phantom
school bus from the past.

$6.95USD/$9.95CDN • ISBN 1-894877-56-X • 4.25" x 7.5" • 144 pages

Horribly Haunted Houses
by Barbara Smith

A wonderful bunch of tales of the unexplained by best-selling ghost stories
writer Barbara Smith, just for kids! Houses are often considered the most
haunted of places and this book makes it clear why. You'll meet young people who live in haunted houses and explore some of the spookiest spaces on
the planet.

$6.95USD/$9.95CDN • ISBN 1-894877-54-3 • 4.25" x 7.5" • 144 pages

Campfire Ghost Stories
by Jo-Anne Christensen

This entertaining collection is sure to raise the hair on the back of your neck.
Read about six glowing orbs of light—the ghostly remains of doomed travelers—that warn campers to leave or face certain death. In another story, a
young girl who grows up with a ghostly double finally discovers the secret
behind her extraordinary doppelganger. And there's much more...

$10.95USD/$14.95CDN • ISBN 1-894877-02-0 • 5.25" x 8.25" • 224 pages

These and many more Ghost House books are available
from your local bookseller or by ordering direct.
U.S. readers call **1-800-518-3541**.
In Canada, call **1-800-661-9017**.